DEATH WIND

❧ A NOVEL ❧

MARGARET F. LAING

Lilac
Publishing

Book cover, interior book design, and eBook design
by Blue Harvest Creative
www.blueharvestcreative.com

DEATH WIND

This book is a work of fiction. The characters, incidents, and dialogue are
drawn from the author's imagination and are not to be construed as real.
Any resemblance to actual events or persons, living or dead, is entirely
coincidental.

Published by
Lilac Publishing

ISBN-13: 978-0-9890981-6-8
ISBN-10: 0989098168

Dedicated to the memory of
CHIEF SITTING BULL
And his
WARRIOR BRAVES

DEATH WIND

The elders of Chief Lone Wolf's tribe sat around the fire, looking from one to the other, talking in low tones, their camp had been raided while they were out hunting. Their women had been abducted, the camp destroyed, teepees burned. Swift Eagle sat off from the others, listening quietly, being respectful of the elders. He sharpened the metal staves his friend, Quint Long Shadow, made for him. Quint was the local black smith in the rural town of Black Water. Quint made them special for Swift Eagle and never ask why or what for. He only ask how many? He just made what his Indian friend asked him to make.

Swift Eagle was a half breed his father, Frank Winthrop, was a white man exploring the west and had come into Chief Lone Wolf's camp. He had fallen in love with, the beautiful Indian maiden, Morning Star. She had cast shy glances at him and he wanted to marry her. Frank ask the chief if she would consent to be his wife. Chief Lone Wolf told Morning Star the white man wanted to marry her and be her husband. She shyly accepted. Chief Lone Wolf gave his consent and performed the marriage ceremonial ritual.

Frank Winthrop was made a blood brother of the tribe. Frank loved his new life. They had two children a son, then a daughter. Frank's parents couldn't understand why their son refused to return home to Boston.

Frank was hunting one day and caught a renegade fur trapper stealing their furs. Frank fought with him knocking him to the ground when Frank turned to collect their furs, the renegade knifed Frank in the back. When he didn't return to camp they began to look for him. The braves found Frank and carried him to the camp he lived long enough to tell them the name of the renegade before he died. Swift Eagle vowed to avenge his father's death.

Time went by nothing was spoken of the renegade, one day while hunting one of the braves, Night Hawk, came upon the skeleton remains. Swift Eagle had avenged his father's death. The skeletal remains were found pinned to a tree with a long stave. Swift Eagle left him there for the wolves and wild animals to devour. Pinned through the pelvis, the renegade couldn't reach the weapon and remove it. He screamed out to the forest. If any renegade heard the sound of death wind, they shivered in fear.

"Aiee, Aiee." Swift Eagle raised his voice having caught the man who killed his father. They knew his sound through the forest and they shuddered in fear trying to hide from him. Many unscrupulous men found they regretted their wicked deeds to the Indians when he caught up to them. He was like a shadow moving silently through the forest. The wind sound from his throat, echoed through the forest. His name was whispered as Swift Eagle, like a howling wolf on the hunt. The sound carried for miles as he began tracking the men who destroyed their camp and abducted the women. The renegades had been warned to leave the Indians alone and stay clear of their camp.

Two of the women abducted were his mother, Morning Star and his sister, Silver Wing. He never said anything, just stood up looked at the braves, and went to the edge of the clearing listening as he looked down at the signs where the renegades tried to brush away their foot prints and the signs of dragging their captives along. He vanished silently disappearing in the forest.

The renegades would sell the girl to men at the trading post and others for furs. The women they would sell at trading posts for servants to be used however they wished to use them. He knew his sister would have been raped by the time they left their camp ground, and he planned to have revenge for *that* first. He moved along silently through the forest, like a shadow his throat naturally gave out the howling wind sound, he could smell the flesh of the trappers.

The man who ran the trading post knew better than to cross Swift Eagle's path. Not many lived after encountering his wrath. The ones who lived after an encounter never forgot it and never wanted to see him again. Swift Eagle let those he knew to be innocent of the crime go free, otherwise their bones would be found rotting against the trunk of a tree, pinned through their groin to the tree. They screamed like their hostages did when they murdered the older women, raped the innocent and killed the infants. "Nits" they had been called by some, if they found the men were off hunting.

The wild animals knew the call of Death Wind. They gathered for the feast when the rapist and murder was so weak he couldn't kick back or wave his arms and they hung by his side the wolves and coyotes closed in. The braves knew Swift Eagle hunted alone, he wanted to find these renegades first, his plan was to find them as a warning for those who would raid and harm their helpless women. Swift Eagle made the sound, "Aiee." when he rendered his justice. Some thought it like a death wind.

Strong Bow and White Wolf with other of the braves moved swiftly and silently through dense forest, following his track, after he disappeared. He could come up and they would never know he was there. After a day tracking the braves heard Swift Eagle's sound echo through the forest. It was faint. They knew he found one of them. The braves slipped along silently toward the sound.

They heard a man's voice, start screaming and yelling, "No, no, help no help".

Then a louder scream and muffled screams as his face smashed into the tree trunk, the metal stave rammed through his groin, pinned him. Swift Eagle sounds again were farther as he moved, swiftly hunting the rest of them.

The renegades were scattered now, scared scrambling wildly over fallen trees and brush, trying to escape the Indian brave. One dropped the stolen furs, the squaw, and the girl in the brush, the renegade could still hear the man pinned to the tree scream. He wasn't waiting to find out if he could help him. Swift Eagle's mother, Morning Star and his sister, Silver Wing were dumped unconscious and bleeding. Swift Eagle stooped down beside his mother, Morning Star, she opened her eyes and looked up at her son.

"I am all right, Son, go fast find Silver Wing."

"Mother, she is here with you," he said and disappeared into the brush. He quickly found their trail and was gone.

The faint screams in the distance could be heard as the rapist and murderer was pinned helplessly, awaiting his final redemption for his evil deed. He soon returned to find his mother and sister. Chief Lone Wolf had come upon his mother. He waited beside Morning Star and Silver Wing.

"You go fast, Swift Eagle, catch the others."

"Me stay here by mother."

"No, Son, you go quickly now. Catch them."

Swift Eagle again, disappeared into the forest following one of the renegades. He wasn't even trying to cover his tracks but running scared, wildly thrashing through the woods, breaking branches, scrambling along falling, and trying to get away from the braves and sounds, he could still hear in the distance. He knew the Indian brave caught him. He scrambled to the lake silently in the water and under some lily pads. Swift Eagle stopped and stood, silent he could see bubbles rising up by the lily pad. He went over reached down, grabbed the man by the throat, dragging him yelling and kicking to a tall cypress tree pushed his face into the tree, thrust the stave quickly through his groin as he yelled loudly.

"I'm sorry I'm sorry Injun, I won't do it again. Help please don't leave me here."

Swift Eagle sort of grunted.

"Ugh, me know you not do it again" these trappers would not rape their daughters and women or destroy their camp again.

The braves also knew the trappers they caught and this one wouldn't do it again. They slipped silently along, tracking the rest of them still dragging some of the women with them to sell at the trading post. Chief Lone Wolf, held Silver Wing unconscious, in his arms rocking to and fro, chanting a prayer to the Great Thunder Bird Spirit. Morning Star leaned against him. They knew the renegades would be found by their braves. The braves didn't pin them to a tree, they pinned them over an ant bed or hung them from a tree branch cut them so they would bleed and draw the wolves and animals to them as they hung helplessly on the branch, just out of reach of the ground, hands bound behind them with raw hide. They showed no mercy knowing what they did to their women and girls. These renegades were told they would be hunted down if they angered the Indians now they were scattered, running wildly, trying to hide, in the woods, and thought of what they had been told at the Fort and trading post about the braves and Swift Eagle. They had heard it now, "Aieee, Aieee", and shivered in fear. The brave could see the remaining reneges were headed toward the trading post and would be there by morning at the pace they were scrambling along.

Swift Eagle knew his brother braves would catch them in the morning at the trading post. There wasn't any place they could hide from them and the soldiers were miles away He ran back to Chief Lone Wolf, Morning Star, and Silver Wing. He lifted his sister in his arm and held his mother. Morning Star clinging to, Chief Lone Wolf could stand and help, they made their way back to their destroyed camp grounds. They would build their home again. Swift Eagle placed Silver Wing gently on a blanket of moss and dipped the moss in the water nearby to sooth her face.

The other braves were trailing the renegades on toward the trading post. They would leave the other Indian women there. They were hoping to escape the brave's anger.

Morning Star was able to stand and help with her daughter now. Chief Lone Wolf had some furs he had dried. He brought poles and set up a teepee then covered it with the fur pelts. He laid Silver Wing in the shade. She regained consciousness and asked for some water, there was a tin can left by the branch, Morning Star, filled the can with cool clean water and gave her daughter a few sips at a time.

Swift Eagle sat by the edge of the branch. He was praying to the Great Thunder Bird Sprit God to help heal his sister, Silver Wing. Later he took the furs Chief Lone Wolf had. He ran to the trading post to exchange them for the supplies needed to care for his mother and sister. The six foot Scotsman Red Beard, knew Swift Eagle and respected him and Chief Lone Wolf's tribe. They were quiet people never causing anyone trouble.

"You tell me what you need, Swift Eagle. You can pay me when you get things in order at your camp."

"Ugh, Red Beard man, we pay now with furs for this."

He only took what the furs would buy, four blankets, coffee, sugar, dried beans, corn meal, salt, flour, and a slab of salted pork belly. He hurried off to help the Chief rebuild their camp. They had the meat they from today's hunt when the camp was not protected by the braves, the meat was in the cold branch water covered and wrapped with leaves. He found it where it had been cooled. The Chief made the fire and cooked some meat making broth to give Silver Wing, she could swallow something now and was showing more strength.

The Scotsman, Red Beard told Swift Eagle the renegades ran by the store, stole his mules. and went off toward the fort. The captain at the fort would know the mules belonged to Red Beard when they got there. He would most likely arrest them and put them under guard. The renegades better hope they got to the fort before the braves or Swift Eagle caught up to them first.

The braves found their women and daughters at the trading post beyond Red Beard's place and left them there. The renegades hoped it would stop the Indians following them.

The braves knew now, they were riding Red Beards mules and heading to the fort. The women at the Dusty Road Trading Post helped the squaws, gave them water, cleaned, and bandaged their wounds and scratches. They gave them something to eat tried and comforting the young girls as best they could. They would keep them safe until the Indian braves returned for them. The braves found the tracks then started running to catch them before they reached the fort and sought protection there. The old Irish man Mick Riley, thought their best hope was to get to the fort before these Indian braves caught up with them, for there won't be a need then.

Swift Eagle knowing his camp was secured with Chief Lone Wolf, ran past the Dusty Road Trading post to catch up to his brothers. They were so close to these renegade, they could smell the mules they were riding. Of course it was the law if you stole either a man's mule or horse you would hang for it. Swift Eagle would rather mete out the Indian justice and let the others understand you don't raid an Indian campground and get away with it. Of course, the government would protect them and let the rogues free. They didn't care what had been done to the Indian women and girls. The braves found them at the fort. They caught the three of them before they got inside the fort. They were found hanging by a limb of a tree, bleeding. The wolves already got them. The soldiers just cut them down knowing they got what they really deserved.

By law they were supposed to hunt the braves down. There was no way they could prove which braves had caught these renegade. The fort would let the others know if they raided an Indian camp and were caught, the fort commander would prosecute them. Swift Eagle wasn't about to depend on fort justice, they let them go and forgot what they had done. He liked the Indian justice best. They never repeated the offense.

When they came on a skeletal remains lying on the ground at the base of a tree, with a hole in the pelvis bone, they knew Swift Eagle had revenge, but had come back for his stave. The only way they could have accused him of the deed. The braves Strong Bow, Night Cloud, and Running Deer herded the mules back to the Dusty Road Trading Post. They took their squaws and daughters home to the camp.

Swift Eagle and Chief Lone Wolf had started putting the camp back together. Morning Star cooked enough stew for the others. The braves cut poles and set up the teepees. They smoked the meat they had and built their fires. They hung blankets over the poles until they had enough animal hide to dry and stretch over their poles.

Silver Wing was up now and able to help around the place. She was ashamed after being raped by the renegades. She was glad she was not going to have a baby from it. Her brother told her the man paid. He screamed for his life, as she had for hers. She was in love with the brave Strong Bow, and now thought he wouldn't want her now as his squaw.

Swift Eagle told his sister that Strong Bow loved her for herself and nothing changed his love for her. She cried and hid in the woods all day. Morning Star worried over her daughter, not because of wild animals with four legs, but now for animals with two legs called man. Swift Eagle told Strong Bow.

"Strong Bow, you come to Swift Eagle camp to talk about Silver Wing."

Strong Bow was in love with her, and wanted her for his squaw. "Swift Eagle, she not talk to me now," Strong Bow told him.

"Her heavy heart now because what bad men do to her."

"Strong Bow, happy she still lives. He loves Silver Wing not lose her."

They didn't see Silver Wing come behind where they were talking, she wiped her tears when she heard Strong Bow talking how much he loved her.

"Come to my fire at night, we talk then." Swift Eagle told Strong Bow. He stood and quickly went to his fire and people. Strong Bow left to hunt, the squirrel would be on the limbs to settle for night he would send his arrow swiftly to have food tonight.

As he walked along thinking of Silver Wing he wasn't watching where he usually did and before he knew it he had stepped into the quick sand pond. The braves were aware of it, but he wasn't paying any heed this time. They had laid a log across the quicksand in case someone did fall in they could hang on to it until someone found them and helped them out. He grabbed the log and the more he kicked the deeper his body sank in it. He started yelling and realized he was so far into the forest they couldn't hear him. He just had to hold on and hope if he didn't get back the braves would search to find him.

At night Swift Eagle wondered why Strong Bow wasn't at his fire. Swift Eagle went to Strong Bow's camp where his mother told him, "Strong Bow was gone all day he not come home."

Swift Eagle took his weapons, bow and arrows, started running where Strong Bows tracks were. He found the places he stopped to kill squirrel, then went on hunting. He ran faster when he thought of the quick sand pond.

He yelled, "Ayee, Ayee. Strong Bow, Ayee Ayee, Strong Bow." He could hear a sound like water splashing. He raced to the quick sand pond and there he found Strong Bow clinging to the log.

"Help me, Swift Eagle. I can't get out, help me."

Swift Eagle crawled out on the log reached and caught Strong Bow by his wrists. He pulled against the suction of the quick sand.

"You not try to help, me pull alone."

Swift Eagle knew it would be best and he would not have to pull against the suction of quick sand.

"You hold on again, Strong Bow, me need to rest"

Swift Eagle stopped and rested a minute, then straddled the log crawling backward holding Strong Bow's wrists again. He pulled Strong Bow along with him. They would rest while Strong Bow would hold to the log Swift Eagle would rest a few minutes then continue pulling him to the edge of the pond. The moon was over head when Swift Eagle came to the edge of the quick sand pond. He stood up and pulled Strong Bow out on the bank of the pond. Strong Bow lay there, catching his breath. Swift Eagle lay by him catching his breath. He looked at his friend and said, "Strong Bow, why you not see quick pond?"

"Me think of Silver Wing, forget pond, and go in it, Swift Eagle."

They lay there until both of them caught their breath and then hurried back to their camp grounds Swift Eagle hailed their camp, "Ayee, Ayee."

The tribe ran to see them come from the forest into the fire light. Strong Bow covered with mud. They sat by the fire in center of the ring of teepee's. The others gathered around and sat waiting to hear the story of why Strong Bow didn't come home. He did find his squirrel though and gave them to his mother.

Silver Wing sat with her mother, Morning Star. They quietly listened as Strong Bow told how he thinking of Silver Wing and fell into the pond of quick sand.

"No one hear me call. Strong Bow keep his strength by holding on the log first with one hand and then change to the other. Strong Bow glad when he see Swift Eagle come from forest to pond. Swift Eagle crawls on log and hold my hand he lay over log crawl back pull to edge of quick pond."

Silver Wing said, "Strong Bow, me happy you here."

Swift Eagle thought it must have been the Great Thunder Bird Spirit God who made this to show Silver Wing, she loved him more and not lose him. Swift Eagle was glad. Now they could go back to hunting and daily life unless, a warring tribe of Indians wanted a battle. He resolved not to leave the camp unguarded from now on.

The Trading Post sent an Indian who worked in the store for Red Beard to tell Swift Eagle of a white man asking about his father and knew his father's name. He told Red Beard (Scotty) Swift Eagle's father was his brother. Swift Eagle really wasn't interested in seeing this white man. His father sat around their camp fire and told stories of his mother, father, and brother. He left and wanted to come out west. They didn't want him to leave their home. He left anyway.

Swift Eagle would think on this. He went off into the forest and sat by the pond thinking he heard someone slipping through the underbrush.

He lay flat with his ear to the ground listening and thought he could see a wisp of white dart through the underbrush. He lay silent knowing it wasn't an animal and not a man or brave. The thing came closer and he could smell it. What was that smell? Sort of like his sister Silver Wing, it couldn't be her. He was startled as he looked through the thick brush into the blue eyes of a white girl long yellow hair, naked. Seeing him, she darted into the brush and disappeared. He forgot all about the white man who was asking about him at Red Beards Trading Post. Who was this girl? She didn't look like his sister Silver Wing, her face was more brown not white like the clouds. Where did she come from? He heard mother speak of settlers long ago coming through this way and being lost. No one could find them. Maybe this was one from the story. He would ask mother when he was back in camp.

Swift Eagle now recalled feeling he was being watched at times when he was deep into the forest, he didn't think anything except it would be a bear cub. He knew it was not a human. Man, he could tell the scent. He did recall a scent during the times he wondered what it was, he guessed the white looking girl had the scent he smelled now. It was her following him through the thick forest, but where did she live? Where was her mother? Did she have a cave to live in? He had many questions now. He knew Chief Lone Wolf would know the stories of the settlers who never were found when they went into the woods toward another place they called Texas.

Swift Eagle hurried back to the camp wanting to talk with Chief Lone Wolf about the white girl he had seen. He called her White Cloud.

He went to the camp. Chief Lone Wolf was sitting by his teepee. Swift Eagle went over to him.

"Chief Lone Wolf, me talk with you at night?"

"Me be here at night fire, come then."

He went back to their teepee and sat with his mother. he asked her about the covered wagon which went by the camp many moons ago. Morning Star remembered the woman was going to have a baby. One of the Indian women helped deliver her baby and they stayed at the trading post until the woman gave birth. When the woman was able to travel, they soon moved on. After they left she knew nothing else of them except a group of soldiers from the fort came to the trading post asking about them, saying they had not arrived at the camp in Texas where they were expected. Swift Eagle was more than ever determined to find the white girl he had seen. He would talk with Chief Lone Wolf about it at the fire tonight.

He went back to the woods where he has been when she came up to where he was. He thought if she were tracking him, she might come again. He lay quietly in the deep brush, waiting and listening to the sounds of the forest and animals. The squirrels chattered and barked in the giant live oak trees, suddenly a quiet came over the woodland. He lay silent hoping the animals had seen something then a wolf howled, it was accompanied by a human sound howling with the wolf. He thought this White Cloud must be with a mother wolf. He laid still waiting, held his knife in case a bear wandered into his hiding place in the tall grass. The stillness was broken by the howling of a wolf. The high sound of a human joined the wolf's howl again. Could it be this White Cloud had been raised by a mother wolf and was still hunting with her?

The sound came closer. He could scent the wolf smell, then the girl scent, like his sister Silver Wing. He knew better than to try and capture White Cloud with the she wolf. He would have to kill the wolf if he tried, because she would protect the girl with her life. He guessed the mother wolf had raised the girl baby when the parents disappeared or what ever happened to them. The wolf must have had cubs and nursed the baby girl with her cubs. He sat thinking silently until the sounds vanished into the forest and he felt he could return to the camp without alarming the wolf and the girl. He had much to talk about with Chief Lone Wolf at his fire tonight.

His sister was gaining more confidence in herself as time had passed. She and her brave, Strong Bow, were making plans to marry.

Red Beard sent the runner again to tell him about the white man asking to meet with Swift Eagle and talk about his brother, Frank, which was Swift Eagle's father. He knew his father stopped corresponding with any of the family members after he became a blood brother to the tribe. He never said anything about his white family except his mother and father objected to him traveling out west. Swift Eagle respected his white father and was bound to seek revenge when he was killed by the rogue he caught stealing his furs. Frank knocked the thief to the ground. Thinking he was unconscious, turned back to pick up his pelts, the thief knifed him in the back, cut his throat, and stole the furs. Braves found Frank and carried him to camp where he told the man's name. After a time Swift Eagle caught the thief and took care of avenging his father.

Well now, here was the white family again trying to see about his father. He knew he would have to meet with him some time. The man left his name and where he was staying at the fort so he could find him.

He was more interested in finding about White Cloud who lived with a wolf other than meeting his father's white brother. She was at least his sister's age he thought, like many moons she was here in the woods. His sister was nineteen years according to the people at the trading post.

After the braves ate and were around their fires, he went to Chief Lone Wolf's fire.

Swift Eagle sat opposite the Chief waiting to be heard.

"Now my brave let your voice be heard. What you talk with Lone Wolf for?"

"Me see white girl in forest with she wolf, you know of white girl?"

Chief Lone Wolf sat silent, smoking his pipe, and looking into the coals of the fire he finally replied, "White settlers have girl papoose in wagon at Red Beard trading post many moons ago. They go in to forest on trail to place they call Texas, they no at Texas. Army soldier come to camp ask of white man. They wait at Texas, white man and woman no get to Texas."

Soldier track trail of wagon but no find, Lone Wolf know of white girl. She a baby at trading post many moons ago." He sat looking at Swift Eagle wondering why he asked of them.

Swift Eagle returned to their teepee. His mother was by their fire, sitting with Silver Wing.

Morning Star looked over at her son and said, "You must go talk to the brother of your father and settle this. He will not leave unless it is done."

He sat quiet looking over at her and finally replied, "Yes, Mother, I will go see the man Brad Winthrop. He leave card at Red Beards trading store. I no read but Red Beard tell me the name."

Swift Eagle had seen white men at the trading post with clothes and shoes. They were clean and talked different. Some of the braves learned some words from the white men, mostly the government men. He bathed in the creek next morning, put on his buck skin clothes, and moccasins He gathered up his bow and arrows then bid his mother good bye telling her he would be going to the fort where the white man called Brad Winthrop was. As Swift Eagle started to leave the trading, post two soldiers rode in on horseback. Swift Eagle looked at them and waited until they came in the trading post.

Red Beard said, "Say men, are you from Fort McKinley?"

They answered, "Yes we are Red Beard Scotsman. Why do you ask?"

"The Indian brave here is going to the fort to find his uncle, Brad Winthrop, and wondered if he is at the fort before he makes the long run there."

The soldiers looked around at Swift Eagle. They could recognize his features were not all Indian, but favored the white man at the fort.

"Yes, the white man, Brad Winthrop is staying there now."

Red Beard then said, "Swift Eagle you can ride one of my mules to the fort?" Scotty knew the brave was very independent and did not want to be indebted to any white man.

The soldiers then spoke between themselves and replied, "Swift Eagle, we could tell Brad Winthrop you would meet with him here at the trading post tomorrow if you wish."

Swift Eagle looked down and was silent a few minutes before answering, "Yes, I meet with the white man here. Yes."

Red Beard was glad that Swift Eagle wasn't going to have the long run to the fort. While his uncle could come by horseback the following day and meet with him here.

The soldiers turned to say something else to the Indian but he had disappeared. "Do you think he will be here tomorrow Red Beard?"

"Yes, this Indian is honorable. His word is true."

The soldiers made out the trading post report for Colonel Wesley at Fort McKinley which was why they were here. The soldiers stopped and had a fresh drink of water from the flowing well out by the branch, which also ran through the Indian camp grounds. They then bid Red Beard good bye and rode down the trail toward Fort McKinley.

Swift Eagle hurried to tell Morning Star, he would see his father's brother the next day.

Swift Eagle then went to hunt for the night meal. He knew the squirrel would be barking and ready to bed down soon. They would have fresh meat and cornmeal cakes tonight. He went into the woods and waited silently by the quick sand pond where Strong Bow had been. There was a rustling in the brush, he waited until a couple of rabbits came to the edge of the pond for water. He got then both with his arrow for their meal tonight. He quickly cleaned the meat wrapped it in a large leaf from the lily pad in the edge of the pond.

He sat a time waiting, silent. He thought White Cloud and her wolf mother may come this way. After a time, he heard their howl off in the distance knowing they would not be coming this way now. He retrieved his fresh meat from the cool water in the pond and hurried home. His mother, was delighted with the meat. They would have rabbit and corn pone baked over the coals tonight.

He went to the side of the camp where the other braves were talking of the White Cloud and the mother wolf. He said nothing. He didn't know the other braves had seen White Cloud with her mother wolf. He didn't want the wolf killed and knew the only way White Cloud would be captured would be to kill the wolf or catch her away from White Cloud. It was hard to find them ever away from one another. He said nothing about her to the other braves. He hoped they wouldn't see her again.

After they finished eating, Morning Star put the things away and came back to talk with her son. "Son, why did you not go see your father's brother today as you told me you would?"

"Mother, the soldiers were at the trading post from the Fort. They said he could ride to the post tomorrow and it would keep me from running all the way to the fort. Which is why me not go to fort. Me see him next day at Red Beard store. His name, Brad Winthrop, like my father name Winthrop, too. Red Beard tell me. So my name Winthrop."

"Yes, my son, Swift Eagle not the only Winthrop?"

"No, Mother, me always Swift Eagle Winthrop if they want me to be. Now Silver Wing is Winthrop. Morning Star be Winthrop now father be Tall Brave Winthrop. I not know him. Morning Star say name only Frank. Yes, Mother, Tall Man Frank Brave tall brave."

"Yes Swift Eagle, father was tall, brave man."

Swift Eagle went to the forest to be alone, he wanted to think of the things his mother said and what the brother of my father, Frank, Brad Winthrop wants what of Swift Eagle.

To be sure, the next day would make a change in his life, his mother' and sister's lives from then on. You see the parents of Brad and Frank owned a ship yard in Boston, It was left in their will when they passed away, Brad and Frank's children would inherit their share of the money which was in stocks drawing a sizeable interest each month. More than Brad or either of them could use. Brad wanted his nephew to have an attorney to handle his portion of his father's estate.

Swift Eagle couldn't sleep that night for thinking of what his father's brother wanted him to do. Was it he wanted to take him to city where father lived to see grandfather of Swift Eagle? He would try and not think of it. At day light he still had not been asleep. He washed in the branch, dressed in his best buckskins, and moccasins. He bid Morning Star and Silver Wing good bye and headed for the trading post. It was only a few miles off. When he got there the others had heard the white man brother of Swift Eagle's father was coming. They wanted to see what he looked like. Swift Eagle wanted to talk with the uncle alone not where braves would hear what they say. Red Beard had a small kitchen where he would suggest to Brad they go there and talk.

5

Swift Eagle went out and sat by the flowing well to wait for his Uncle Brad. It wasn't long until he could hear horse hoofs against the ground, pulling the buggy along the woods road. He went inside to wait.

Brad pulled the horse up to the hitching rack, threw the reins over it, stepped down, and stood a moment looking toward the door of the Dusty Road Trading Post, wondering if his Indian nephew would be there to meet him. The Scotsman, Red Beard, told Swift Eagle he and his uncle could meet in his kitchen off from the store where they could talk privately without others listening to their conversation. Brad opened the door and walked in. The Indian stood by the counter waiting.

Swift Eagle looked toward the door wondering what Brad Winthrop would look like. As Brad came into the store, the Indian couldn't believe this wasn't his father, Frank, who walked in. He was six feet tall. Uncle Brad looked over his way. He walked over and said, "Ah, yes, hello, you must be

Swift Eagle my brother's son." Brad extended his hand to Swift Eagle, who having seen the soldiers shake hands he reached out and gripped Brad's hand.

"Yes, I am Swift Eagle, brother of my father, Tall Strong Man."

They followed Red Beard noticing the other braves waiting to listen to what they would say to each other. He went over to the white man who just came in the door. "Good morning sir" he looked in the Indians' direction. "Yes, Mr. Winthrop, I have a room where the two of you can speak without others listening to your conversation, come, follow me." Brad came over to Swift Eagle and motioned him to follow. The brave followed and muttered a grunt like the Scotsman they went to the small room.

There was a table, four chairs, and a wood stove in the room.

"Come sit and visit here, I will make coffee. He put the pot on the stove, filled it with water, and coffee. He opened the door of the wood stove and stoked the fire. It would soon have the water boiling. He then returned to the store leaving the two men alone.

Brad sat at the end of the table, Swift Eagle pulled the chair out and sat back from the table looking at this man. He placed his bow and arrows across the top of the table. Brad took notice of it.

"Oh yes, I have not learned the ways of my brothers son. I hope you will show me, Swift Eagle."

Swift Eagle could not get over looking at this man. The way he spoke was like his father, Frank brave Man.

"You want me show you to hunt, brother of my father?"

"Not exactly Swift Eagle, I just didn't know how you hunted for game."

"Me hunt with arrow and bow or with knife for food for mother and sister, Silver Wing."

"I would like to meet you mother and sister if they would like to meet with me, Swift Eagle."

"I talk with mother if she will meet brother of her husband."

'I would like it, Swift Eagle."

"Why, brother of my father, want to talk with Swift Eagle?"

"What I want to talk with Swift Eagle is about much wampum or money, you have from your great grandmother and great grandfather Winthrop of you. They left much money or wampum for you and Silver Wing."

The Indian sat silent, it hadn't yet sunk in what this man said. He knew what wampum meant it was like gold or wampum the traders get for furs he bring to trading post. How this grandmother and grand gather leave him this they not have furs?

Brad realized the Indian didn't comprehend what he was saying, perhaps the Scotsman could help the young man understand.

"Wait a minute, Swift Eagle, I get Red Beard help me tell you." Good lord, here he was talking now like his Indian nephew. He went to the door and asked Scotty if he could come in for a few minutes.

The runner who worked for the Scotsman would tend the post until he could see what this man wanted. He came into the room looked over at the Indian sitting away from the table. He found the coffee ready, he poured each of them a cup, and offered canned cream and sugar to Brad. He knew the Indian drank his black. He pulled up a chair and sat at the table with Brad looked at him and said, "Yes, Mr. Winthrop, what is it you wish of me?" He sipped his coffee waiting for his reply.

Swift Eagle took his cup blowing on the cup to cool the brown liquid.

Brad paused a moment then began, "You see, Scotty, my brother inherited a large amount of money and holdings when our grandparents died. It is now my place to see that my brother's children get the money rightfully theirs. Most of it is in holding bringing in a huge amount of money each month from interest. I have contacted an attorney in Boston to be sure their holdings are properly taken care of and they are not duped into losing their inheritance from some crook."

"Oh yes, now I understand, Brad." He thought well since I am now Scotty, I guess I can call him Brad. He turned to Swift Eagle and said, "Swift Eagle what your uncle Brad wants you to know is you and Silver Wing are wealthy people now."

"What this wealthy mean to Silver Wing and Swift Eagle?"

"It means you can buy what you want without having furs to trade, you now have paper in the bank where Brad lives to use to trade for food, clothes, buckskins, moccasins, anything, even white man clothes and white man moccasins if you want. You and Silver Wing have an Indian teach you to talk like white man talk."

"What you mean Indian teach white man talk?"

Brad then said, "Yes, Swift Eagle, there is an Indian Brave in Boston who can teach you and your sister more words than you know. You not forget Indian words either, just learn more words. It will help you and mother to have good things, even have a cabin house with a window and door, not Teepee to live in."

"What you mean cabin house be mothers. White man no take it from mother?"

"Yes, Swift Eagle, exactly what I mean. The house would be for your mother and sister to have and live in."

The Indian finished the coffee and placed the cup back on the table he sat looking at the two men saying nothing. Not believing what they had told him. He was still thinking how this man was like his father. He couldn't stop looking at him thinking of his father.

Brad then said, "Swift Eagle, tell Morning Star and Silver Wing what you have heard today. Take the time to understand you are now a very rich man. Do you know what rich means?"

Swift Eagle looked at Brad, "Me not know word rich mean."

"Rich means more wampum and fur skins than you could put in trading post store now."

"You say furs and wampum like paper money like Red Beard have in box?'

"Yes, Swift Eagle, like Red Beard has in box. You have many more papers than Red Beard, you can buy Red Beard store if he sell to you."

Swift Eagle sat looking lost. This was too much for this Indian to grasp at this time.

Brad then said, "You take me to your camp so I can meet your mother and sister now?"

"You come to see mother next day, Uncle Brad Winthrop."

"All right I will come tomorrow and see your mother and sister. You know they are my family too, Swift Eagle. I am white man, but Frank Winthrop my blood brother. We are blood family; you and your sister are my blood family."

Scotty thought *hey this old Irishman Brad, will be talking like this Indian, if he hangs around him.* Red Beard thought *well I never thought a halfbreed could one day buy me out if he wanted but for dang sure this Indian could do it.*

• • • • •

Swift Eagle got up and went to the other room. The braves were still there waiting to see what the white man looked like.

Swift Eagle silently went to the door running across the creek to the woods and disappeared. Brad came out and talked with Scotty a few minutes. He went outside, stood there a while, then climbed back in the buggy, turned the rig around, and started back to the fort for the night. He would return in the morning to meet Morning Star and Silver Wing.

Riding along his thoughts turned to this young Indian nephew of his. He was a fine looking man. His brother would have been proud to have seen his son grown to manhood. Brad was hoping he could have influence on him so he and his sister would understand how important an education would be for them. He knew they didn't want to lose their heritage of the Native American Indian. He didn't want them to lose their background and ancestry either. Well, there is much to talk about tomorrow with his mother. I will now see my brother's wife. We always wondered why he chose the Indian maid. There had been a lovely young girl infatuated with Frank in college. His brother was polite to her and took her to dances, dining, and the theater. When it came to marriage, he headed to the west to find what he had missed in school and college. They knew he was happy. His mother and dad missed him, but were happy for their son. They hoped also to meet his wife and children. All these thoughts were going through his mind as he rode along. He soon found himself at the fort, pulled up to the hitching rack, a soldier took the reins. Brad climbed down and went to his room at the fort. He had a wash basin and poured water from the pitcher to the basin on the table, washed the dust off, dried his face and hands, ready to join the officers for dinner.

The colonel invited Brad to eat at the officers' mess hall. He quickly went to dinner not wanting to be late. The meal was just being served, as he sat down at the table. The officers nodded in recognition to him. This was a long way from dining at the lodge in Boston; he rather liked it, and was grateful he was accepted by the men here.

The dinner was great northern beans seasoned with hog fat and fried salt pork, scorched gravy, fresh baked biscuits, wild blackberry jam, and hot coffee. After he finished eating, they went out side to sit and enjoy the cool of the evening. Colonel Wesley naturally was curious what Mr. Winthrop thought after meeting his Indian nephew. He came and sat beside Brad.

"Good evening, Mr. Winthrop, I hope you met your half breed nephew today." Brad knew the man didn't mean anything wrong, it was their ignorant way of describing an Indian who were half white.

"Yes, Sir, I did. He is quite an impressive young gentleman." The colonel looked over at him when he said gentleman, apparently he hadn't heard of this young man's vengeance on those who killed his father and raped his sister.

"I guess now you will be leaving to return to Boston?" The colonel couldn't think a civilized white man would want to stay any longer with the Indians.

"No, Colonel, I will meet my sister-in-law tomorrow. Her name is Morning Star, and also my niece Silver Wing. I am looking forward to meeting them, I could see my family resemblance in Swift Eagle. He resembles my brother, Frank."

Colonel Wesley could hardly believe this man, didn't he know these Indians were savages. Well, no matter he thought best not to say anything about how the skeletal remains were found after Swift Eagle caught up to them recently, after the renegade raided their camp, dragged his mother off with the other women, and his sister was raped, well he thought, It was best to let sleeping dogs lay. Colonel Wesley cleared his throat, pulled his pipe from the pouch, filled it with crimp cut tobacco, lit it, settled back, and smoked looking out beyond the parade grounds.

Brad thought I hope this ignorant bastard understands now, these people, are my family members. He sat silent a while then stood up and said.

"Well Colonel, goodnight, I will see you at breakfast."

"Uh, oh yes, Winthrop, goodnight." The colonel answered.

He went to his room, read the Holy Bible, a few passages from Psalms, 91 and 23 placed his Bible back in his satchel on the chair by the bunk. He then lay down and quickly fell asleep. He would rise early with the soldiers' horn blowing, have breakfast, then take the horse and buggy, and go to Red Beards trading post. He hoped to meet his new found family.

The bugler sounded his horn. It seemed he had no more than gone to sleep. He hurried took his shaving cup to the water pump, lathered his beard, and shaved with his straight razor, quickly stowed it in his satchel.

He hurried to the mess hall hoping not to be late. Fortunately the cook had just placed the fried sow belly, scorch gravy, grits and biscuits on the table. The men served them selves, and passed the food around. Winthrop finished eating, and went to the front where one of the soldiers had the horse and buggy waiting. He handed the reins to Winthrop, and stepped back.

"Thank you," The corporal saluted.

"Good day to you sir." He said.

"Good day to you, Corporal." Brad answered, slapping the reins against the horse's neck, clicked to him, as the horse began trotting out the gate of the fort, and down the woods road toward the Trading Post.

The sun was just clearing the trees, the air was fresh and the trip would only take about an hour or so. Thinking he saw someone ahead in the bushes, he leaned down to look closely, all of a sudden he realized it was a black bear, the horse went

frantic, reared up, and started to run away, Winthrop fortunately had been used to the horse and buggy in Boston, he
held the reins tight, keeping the horse under his control,
talking to him, and finally getting him calm to a trot again.
Whew, he thought, I *didn't bring a rifle with me I only have my
forty four. Well, it's fine now.* He traveled on to the Trading Post
and pulled up to the hitching rack. Scotty was waiting with a
pot of fresh hot coffee.

"Good mornin' to ye, Brad, come in."

"Ah yes, Scotty, good to see you this morning." Before
Scotty could pour Brad a cup of coffee, Swift Eagle came in the
door. They both turned his way.

"Come in, Swift Eagle, the coffee is ready have a cup."

Swift Eagle came to the counter and put sugar in his coffee. This was really a treat. They did without some things to
save and buy other things with their furs.

The three men sat quietly savoring the coffee, this was
chicory flavored, less expensive than the whole grain coffee.
Red Beard (Scotty) tried to keep the expenses down for the
sake of the Indians. Swift Eagle placed the cup on the counter
looked at Winthrop and said, "We go now. You meet mother,
Mooring Star and sister. Silver Wing?"

"Yes, Swift Eagle, I am ready to go. Will we go in the
buggy?" Scotty looked over amazed. This man didn't realize it
was only a foot path to the teepees and camp grounds.

"No, Uncle Brad Winthrop, we go walk in woods to
camp ground."

"Oh, yes, well I didn't know come on lets go." He went to
the door turned and looked at Scotty.

"Would you turn the horse in the corral and feed it until I
return?' He came back to the counter and placed money on the
counter to pay for the feed.

"Aye, I'll see to yer horse, Brad, me friend." Red Beard thought, *This should be an interesting meetin for this man from Boston. At least he is some kind of a regular fellow and has the manner of his brother, Tall Brave Man Frank.* Swift Eagle waited at the edge of the forest for Brad.

"Uncle Brad Winthrop, you stay with Swift Eagle." He started running Brad having been on the swim team and ran some in college was all right with it. He kept right along with his nephew. It did, however seem as if they would never get to the camp. Finally, Brad could see smoke in the trees. They came into the cleared space where people were sitting at the fire in the center. Swift Eagle went to the fire turned and waited for Brad. As they stood there Brad waited for the nephew to do whatever it was he had in mind. The braves sat away from Chief Lone Wolf, who sat waiting to hear from Swift Eagle. Brad was getting a little edgy with the silence.

Swift Eagle then said, "Chief Lone Wolf and brother braves, this man is Tall Strong Man Frank's blood brother."

Brad just stood waiting.

Chief Lone Wolf broke the silence, "Brother of Tall Strong Man come sit by me we smoke pipe together." Brad knew it was the Indian tradition to smoke what was known as a peace pipe. He didn't use tobacco , but would use it today. He went over and sat on the ground by Chief Lone Wolf. He waited while the Chief took a drag from the pipe then handed it to him. Brad put it to his mouth. The tobacco nicotine made him dizzy just smelling it, but he took a draw on the pipe blew the smoke out without inhaling it then gave the pipe to Chief Lone Wolf.

"You look like blood brother Tall Strong Man."

The braves sat watching Frank's brother Swift Eagle's resemblance, with this white man. After a few minutes of being silent Swift Eagle went to his teepee and came back with two women. They came over to the fire and stood facing Chief Lone Wolf and Brad. Nothing was said until Brad broke the silence. He stood up and walked to where Morning Star was. He looked at Silver Wing and could see his brother Frank in her features and skin color. He spoke up loud enough for all to hear him. "Wife of my brother Frank, I am happy to see you." She said nothing just looked at him. He then turned to Silver Wing. "Daughter of my brother Frank, I am happy to see you and know you are like my brother. I see him in your face." She looked down at the ground.

They all were silent' Finally Swift Eagle said, "Uncle Brad Winthrop, brother of my father come let us go to my teepee and talk. They walked to the edge of the woods the women following. They sat in a circle around his fire.

"Brother of my father, tell mother and sister about how we now rich she have cabin house window, door, white man no can make her leave"

Brad wasn't exactly sure how to explain the inheritance to the women.

"You see, Morning Star and Silver Wing, I have much wampum belonging to your Tall Brave Man Frank which now belongs to you."

"Why it belongs to me, you say?"

"Well yes, believe me it is your wampum." The women looked at Swift Eagle expecting him to explain. Well how could he when he didn't understand himself? They just sat looking at each other.

Morning Star said to Swift Eagle, "Bring the squir-rel. I cook. we eat." Swift Eagle was gone a short while and returned with four squirrels on a stick which he gave to Morn-ing Star she hung them over the coals to roast while she mixed up some corn meal and made patties to bake over the coals in a cast iron frying pan with a cover. They sat more or less just looking and listening to the sounds of the woods while the food cooked. Brad told them about the train and the schools in Boston. How they could learn to talk different and make numbers like Red Beard did on paper with a stick of wood. He tried to explain they could to do this and he would help show them. Swift Eagle had been turning the squirrel and the meat sizzled and turned brown, it smelled delicious. Brad thought. he didn't see any dishes and wondered about holding the hot meat to eat. Well to his surprise Morning Star went to the tee-pee and back with four tin plates and forks like the army standard. She placed a squirrel on each one and a patty of corn meal bread. They sat holding the plate.

Swift Eagle took his last then said. "Eat brother of my father. This is good. I catch today before I come to Red Beard to see you."

Brad pulled one of the tender leg quarters from the body and tasted it. He looked at them and said, "Um, this is delicious I like this meat, Swift Eagle. Thank you, Morning Star and Silver Wing."

They looked at each other and sort of smiled. Silver Wing couldn't keep from peeking at this man, because he made her think of her father, who looked like Uncle Brad.

"You stay here tonight, brother of my father. I fix blanket by the fire for you."

"Yes, I will stay. Swift Eagle, today on path the bear came after my horse. I wait until next day, not go at night. I will go to Boston, then come again and bring men to build house for my brother s wife and daughter."

Brad knew his nephew or niece didn't have education enough to have a bank account to handle yet. He hoped he could encourage his Indian friend in Boston to return with him and help out here with his family. He knew they would understand each other better than him trying to explain. Also, he wasn't going to have them taken advantage of by some smart shyster.

He thought his mother would be happy to see her granddaughter, she was a pretty girl. Brad had been married but didn't have children and his wife didn't like living in Boston. He tried going with her to make a living in Alaska where her parents lived. It didn't work out for either of them, they divorced. Brad returned to Boston working with his dad's business in the ship yard. They had numerous holdings and when their parents died and left to Frank's children, it gave them all something to think about.

They had letters from Frank, but hadn't really gotten into looking for them until now. Well, he would have much to tell his mother and father when he returned. He knew his mother would want to come and meet her grandchildren, but he knew the nearest place for her to stay was at least sixteen miles from the Trading Post. He would think of something. It could be he might get them to come to Black Water and stay with her at the hotel for a time and get acquainted with them. He would just have to wait and see.

The evening was cool, the camp fires burned all night, birds in the trees, squirrel chattering in the morning, Swift Eagle was gone when he got up. He stretched to get the kinks out from sleeping on the ground. He could see Morning Star had coffee and was sitting by the fire as if waiting for him. He went to the branch washed his face to wake up, dried on his shirt tail, then came to the fire, she offered him a cup of coffee. It was in a tin cup and very hot. Brad sat on the ground by her. Before long Swift Eagle returned and she gave him coffee. He had rabbits for their meal today. Swift Eagle knew the father's brother Brad was going back to Boston today.

He said, "I will go with you, Uncle Brad Winthrop, to the fort and not have bear come after horse on way to fort."

Brad thought this man wasn't thinking of the long trek he would have to run getting back to the trading post after leaving him at the fort. There was a stage coach coming to the fort on the weekend, he could leave then to catch the train to home.

Brad said, "Good bye, Morning Star and Silver Wing, I am happy I know you now. I will return and things will be better for you. Then I will bring help to build a house for you to live in. He knew it would be difficult with the damned red tape the government put the Indians through.

Well maybe he could find some way to get his sister in law into a house and more comfort. He knew this was their way of life because it was all they knew or ever had.

Brad followed Swift Eagle through the path to the trading post. Scotty had the horse hitched to the buggy waiting and they were on the way in no time. Swift Eagle left Brad and returned to his camp.

Swift Eagle turned at the edge of the forest and began running along the path into the woods road, soon disappearing into the forest, to return to his teepee home.

Brad returned safely to the fort without any further incident on the woods road leaving the horse with the corporal he went into his room washed up, shaved, packed his few things in his satchel, closed it, and was ready to board the stage coach when it came through.

Brad went to dinner with the soldiers and of course every now and then the cook would have venison either fried or a nice stew of meat, potatoes onion, and gravy. Depending on if the supplies had come in. Usually it was the stew without anything but biscuits to soak up the delicious gravy. Brad tried to spend the time waiting for the stage coach by walking around the parade grounds not venturing outside the gate, because of the wild animals, not Indians, a person had to fear these days. Actually Brad knew the Indians had reason to be defensive, the white man had taken over his hunting grounds, destroyed their camps, defiled the women, and even murdered their women and children. Sitting Bull sort of evened the score he thought. His brother's children were his now and he would defend them.

Swift Eagle returned to the Dusty Road Trading Post by noon. He was ready to have some of the flowing sulphur water from the well by the corral. He leaned down drinking, then settled on the ground by the corner of the corral. Red Beard seeing him come up went out by him. Swift Eagle looked up at him.

"You want a cup of coffee, Swift Eagle?" Red Beard ask him.

Swift Eagle sat looking up at him a few minutes then replied, "No, Red Beard, father's brother, Uncle Brad Winthrop said you have wampum from my money for me?"

"Yes, I have wampum to give you what you want, Swift Eagle?"

"Swift Eagle want Red Beard make box of food with hog fat, salt fat meal, coffee, sugar, salt, you fix box for food plate's, blankets, you fix three boxes for Morning Star."

Then Red Beard asked him. "Would you want some calico cloth, for a woman dress not buckskin?"

"Swift Eagle ask mother. Morning Star me tell you when me come for other boxes."

Red Beard fixed two boxes with everything he thought Swift Eagle's mother would like to keep her home in order. When Swift Eagle returned, Red Beard was surprised to see him with a drag to carry the extra boxes on. Red Beard helped him load them and watched as he pulled it on to the pathway to their camp.

• • • • •

Morning Star told Swift Eagle she had seen White Cloud sneaking and peeking through the bushes at her and his sister, Silver Wing, she missed some of the buckskin dresses she made Silver Wing and moccasins.

"Mother Morning Star, was the girl, White Cloud, with her wolf mother?'

"No, she alone, Swift Eagle, the wolf mother not with White Cloud she must be dead. White Cloud watches Silver Wing and do yellow hairs back like Silver Wing do hair."

She leaned down on the ground and crawled away so I not see her go in forest."

"I will look for White Cloud. Me no want brother braves find White Cloud girl, the mother wolf may be gone or dead."

Morning Star and Silver Wing were busy placing the dishes and food that Swift Eagle had in the boxes. She was happy Tall Brave Man Frank's blood brother, Brad Winthrop, was here and gave the food. Of course, they never realized it was Swift Eagle and Silver Wings rightful inheritance. Well, there was enough money to keep them for several years left there with Red Beard. Brad told him where to write and let him know if the money was gone so he would be sure his family there didn't go without food and the necessities for their lives and well-being. He had set up a trust fund and hired an attorney to help keep their money invested for their future.

Now that Swift Eagle knew White Cloud was watching their camp and his sister, he wanted to find where she stayed all the time with her wolf mother.

"Mother, I will be away for two moons. I will find the White Cloud girl and see where she stay with wolf mother den. Red Beard have my rich wampum at trading store you get what you want now."

Morning Star watched her son disappear into the forest, he wanted to see this white girl with the yellow hair and her wolf mother. The squaws couldn't help being jealous of Morning Star, because she had all these things.

What she did was to share the things she had with them. Then the ladies of the camp were happy. They wrapped in the new blankets and sang songs while sitting around the fire waiting for the braves to return with fresh meat. Peace reined in Chief Lone Wolf's tribe.

Silver Wing made some moccasins now with bright beads on the top of them. She had forgotten her cruel treatment by the renegade who abducted her. The score settled by her brother, Swift Eagle. She wondered about him if he found White Cloud's den where she was with her wolf mother. Would he bring her to the camp to be her sister? Strong Bow had seen her when he was caught in quick sand. She came there to drink water and wash food, he saw tracks when rescued brother brave, Swift Eagle heard the brush moving, quietly watching, White Cloud came to the pond.

The white girl slowly came up to the edge of the pond, she paused waiting, listening silent still looking first one way the other way, slowly kneeled to the ground, finally laying flat, she leaned to the water sipped it slowly drinking, paused raise her head listening Swift Eagle thought, the mother wolf had taught her well.

He waited, after she finished drinking and started to raise up. Swift Eagle grabbed her shoulders holding her down until she calmed down.

He just held her strongly to the ground so she couldn't run away. Swift Eagle raised his head and howled as he had seen her mother wolf do. White Cloud looked sideways at him wondering what kind of animal this was. He felt her relax, but didn't let his hold on her go. He wondered if she knew Indian talk. She was wearing Silver Wings clothes and moccasins He thought a moment and said, "Swift Eagle not hurt white girl."

She stopped resisting and was quiet a minute, then to his surprise she said, " Mama, not hurt mama, not hurt." She turned her head trying to look up at his face.

"Me not hurt let go, me not hurt let go." He didn't understand what she was trying to say but thought if he let her go she would disappear into the woods, and it would be forever until he saw her again. He held her and tried to keep talking to her different words, he then remembered the white man say they wrote with a stick in what they said a Bible and the stick put a name in the Bible. He said, "Mama, not hurt you Bible." She seemed excited when he said the word Bible.

"Bible, Bible, mama, Bible, Bible," she said again. "Mama, Bible."

These words seemed to be understood by this white girl. She had to be the girl baby who was at the trading post many moons gone now. He decided to release his hold slightly, but kept a grip on her arms. He knew she could bite him as a wolf did but he released her and held her arms. She rose up looked at his face. She had one of Silver Wings buckskin dresses on. He knew now where they had disappeared. She looked at him wondering what kind he was, not white like she was, but brown like the ones in the camp. They just sat looking at each other. Swift Eagle raised his head, "Wahoo! Wahoo."

He raised his head and made the wolf howl again. She sat silent a minute and raised her head and howled as he had seen her do some time ago by the pond. White Cloud no longer was trying to break free from Swift Eagle. She realized he wasn't trying to hurt her. She pulled her arms away from him and said, "Mama no hurt."

He released her arms and sat back. He waited wondering now what would this white girl do. She slowly sat up crossed her legs and sat Indian style, staring at him.

He stood up, she backed away, he said, "Mama no hurt."

She stood staring not trying to run. He motioned like her to follow him. He started back toward their camp. After a few steps, he stopped and looked to see if she was following him. She was coming along but hiding behind bushes as she followed him. He wondered if she would come to his teepee or shy away. Morning Star would be like a Bible mama not hurt.

They went on it was a good eight miles to his teepee. When they came closer, White Cloud stopped, and was saying.

"Bible mama not hurt, mama not hurt?" This time it was like a question. Swift Eagle stopped turned, and looked at her then said, "Me, Bible mama not hurt." She somehow must have gotten his message. When they got to the edge of the camp he went around to the back of his teepee. She stopped just stood there waiting.

He called softly, "Mother, Morning Star, I have the white girl come back of teepee. Tell girl, "Mama no hurt she know."

They waited and soon Morning Star slowly came around the teepee, the girl crouched back. Morning Star said softly, "Mama no hurt. Mama no hurt."

The girl came forward to look at Morning Star. They stood looking at each other. Silver Wing came there with them. She stood looking at the white girl wearing her buckskins. Silver Wing came forward toward her and reached out her hand to the white girl, who just stood looking a minute, and then reached and touched Silver Wing's hand. She motioned the girl to come with her. The white girl stepped carefully to the teepee, stood waiting, looking around at the rest of the teepees, and women in front of them. She had seen them when she had taken the buckskin dress but wasn't sure what they would do to her. Morning Star came with her and Silver Wing to teepee. She opened the door flap and beckoned White Cloud to come with them. She saw blanket on ground, White Cloud quickly settled down on it, and fell asleep as if she felt safe and was exhausted. Morning Star smiled at the sleeping girl, then went outside to Swift Eagle He was sitting by their fire.

"Mother, is White Cloud girl scared?"

"White Cloud girl, sleep on Silver Wing blanket."

He went, looked, and saw the girl asleep on Silver Wing's blanket.

"She tired and not scared." He wondered where her mother wolf was. It must have been killed, or it would have been with the white girl. He would find the place her mother wolf was. If she would show him where he could find her Bible book, mother no hurt. The soldiers never found the wagon anywhere in the forest, they must have fallen it quick sand or something happen to Mother no hurt.

Morning Star was busy fixing some meat with potatoes for them. She knew White Cloud wouldn't remember eating like this. The wolf mother took the infant baby girl as one of her cubs. She didn't remember the way her parents used the forks or spoons.

9

She would have to watch them eat to learn how to eat from a bowl or hold a tin spoon. The meat smelled delicious, Swift Eagle was hunting when White Cloud girl awakened and came out with Morning Star. She recognized her as a Bible no hurt mama. She sat by Silver Wing and watched everything around the camp. Morning Star gave her a whole cake of corn meal pone. She devoured it. Morning Star could see she was hungry. She filled a bowl and gave it to Silver Wing. White Cloud watched as Silver Wing took the tin spoon and dipped the food, blowing it to cool it then tasted it. She looked over at White Cloud offered the bowl and spoon to her. White Cloud slowly took them and tried dipping the spoon, it fell off at first, but finally she began eating like a starved wolf. Morning Star took the bowl and filled it again. This time the White Cloud girl waited for the stew to cool. She was looking at them, wondering all the time shaking, and trembling in a calm fear while watching the others.

Morning Star took her hand and said, "Bible mama no hurt." She repeated it to Morning Star.

Silver Wing went to her and sat by her taking her hand, pressed it against her shoulder, and said," Me, Silver Wing." The girl watched as Morning Star did the same thing. White Cloud tried to form the words. Morning Star put her hand on White Cloud.

"You my daughter, White Cloud." She looked at her and tried to say the words.

It would be some time until this girl learned to trust, listen to the tribe women. and form the words. She watched Silver Wing and copied the things she did.

One day Swift Eagle decided it was time to find White Cloud's Bible Mama and where the mother wolf was. He wondered if the girl would show then the way to the wolf den. Swift Eagle thought the girl would follow his sister.

Silver Wing took her hand and walked in back of her brother into the forest. They went along and White Cloud watched where they were going. She would pull away and show a different pathway, the bushes were sort of mashed down where they had been walked on. Swift Eagle found some of the wolf's hair on brush by the path. He stopped, stooped down pulled the hair from the bush. White Cloud raised her head and gave her wolf howl, "Aiee, aiee."

Swift Eagle also did his wind howl to keep her from being frightened at finding her mother wolf's hair. She pulled to another path, bending down under some low branches, the path continued on toward the thick forest. Swift Eagle saw what looked like the marks a buggy wheel made on the road to the fort. They walked on until dark.

Swift Eagle stopped under a huge live oak tree, he cleared away the under brush, and started a fire. Silver Sing sat down beside the fire, White Cloud also copied her looking at Swift Eagle wondering what he was doing. He disappeared and soon returned with squirrels he had them on three stout sticks which he secured in the ground leaning over the fire. After eating they lay down to sleep for the night. He kept the fire bright and warm all during the night.

They awakened at daylight, he found a creek, the three lay down and drank from the cold, clear, flowing spring-fed creek. The wheel marks still showed on the trail she was leading them along. This overgrown path where the ruts had gone down into the soil. Another day passed, Swift Eagle had two rabbits he killed with his bow and arrows, again he roasted them over a fire wrapped them in leaves and covered the leaves with the coals. When the rabbit was done he gave each of them a portion of the meat. They walked on.

White Cloud became edgy and excited saying, "Bible Mama, Bible mama."

They soon found where the wagon tracks ended. There in front of them were the remains of the ragged, tattered, covered wagon. White Cloud ran to it reached and showed them the worn leather Bible,

"Bible mama, Bible mama." Swift Eagle knew if his Uncle Brad Winthrop saw the Bible he would read Bible out loud. He would bring Bible book to the camp. Silver Wing climbed inside the wagon, it creaked with her light weight, and she stood looking where a blanket had been on the floor, there were some pans and tin plates on the floor, a baby cradle with wolf hairs clinging to it. She pointed to it.

White Cloud raised her head, "Whoeeee, whoeeee." Howling as her wolf mother did.

They knew the mother wolf had been in the cradle at some time. Swift Eagle wondered what happened to the mother and father of girl. He looked the wagon and found a mound of sand and rocks on top. This was mama or father of girl. As he looked around again he found the skeleton remains of another person. The shreds of clothes on it were men's.

There were ashes with a spit over it and a pot hanging there. White Cloud went over to it, put her fingers inside the pot, and then licked them. Someone must have cooked there and she remembered. She stood there as if thinking, then said, "Papa eat, Papa, eat."

She dipped her fingers in the pot again. She looked inside the wagon, there were a few dried lima beans still, scattered and whole grains of corn the squirrels had missed. A sack which said corn meal on it, Swift Eagle recognized it from the Trading Post.

Well, he had found her wagon, now where was her wolf mother? Swift Eagle put the Bible in his quiver to take back when they returned to their camp. He would ask Red Beard to read it for him.

White Cloud went toward an opening in the bushes. They followed her to the place where the wolf had died in her den. White Cloud raised her head again and howled, like the wolf mother.

Swift Eagle also raised his head and howled he then touched her arm and motioned her to follow. They now must return to their camp. It had been now almost four days since they left. Swift Eagle now could tell Red Beard where the wagon was and he would tell the soldiers from the fort.

They started back and slept near the quick sand pond one night, then the next two nights near the branch where he caught the renegade. The bones had fallen to the ground, he picked up his metal stave and put it with the others in the quiver on his back.

White Cloud looked at the skeleton and walked on with them knowing what had happened to him. She was hiding in the brush. She had watched when Swift Eagle caught the renegade. White cloud was hiding and watching when renegades raided their camp and what the men did to Silver Wing. Swift Eagle soon caught him she thought.

Her memory of her Papa and the wagon where she had lived with her Bible mother and Papa were coming to her. She would say, "Papa." while they were walking then,

"Papa cook and me eat. Mama no eat. Mama in ground." She was putting some words together.

Swift Eagle was listening, trying to understand, but said nothing. Red Beard would be surprised when he learned about the wagon and the girl. Swift Eagle knew men who hunt buffalo see girl, try catch her. At dusk they went into camp, the fires were burning in front of the teepees, Swift Eagle raised his head and yelled, "Aiee, aiee."

Morning Star knew they had returned. They joined her at the teepee and fire. She was glad they were home.

"Mother, we find wagon. Girl finds mama in ground, find wolf mother, no live now she in den.

White Cloud was watching and listening raised her head and said, "Whoee, whoee," howling like her wolf mother. She then sat near the fire her head down.

"Me have. Mama Bible no hurt. Uncle Brad Winthrop read Bible when he comes?"

He gave the Bible to Morning Star who opened it and saw picture of man and woman. She put book in the teepee by the moccasins. Swift Eagle knew his uncle Brad could read it when he returned from the place he called Boston.

• • • • •

Little did they know he would be coming back the next year bringing lumber and carpenters. Brad had ask Red Beard if he could build a house on his land. He knew the government wouldn't let Morning Star have her own land. This would give her safety though on his land. He would pay the Scotsman a handsome price for it and put it in his name. This would be his brother's widow and children's home. He had a wood stove along with the lumber, a pitcher pump, and enough pipe to put a well down by the house. Of course, an outdoor privy also. Brad consulted with his dad's attorneys having their inheritance invested wisely so they wouldn't ever want for anything. He hoped the girl and Swift Eagle would agree to come with him to Boston live with them and attend a private school so they could have special teaching and not be subject to ridicule by ignorant white people. Well, he would cross that bridge when he got to it.

• • • • •

Silver Wing and White Cloud became friends, she let the other girls of the tribe know her and about where they found her Mama Bible and Papa. The others were curious, but kind to the strange white girl. Morning Star thought it best to darken her white yellow hair because of the buffalo hunter, she also rubbed berry dye on her face, arms and hands to make them dark like theirs.

White Cloud now was calling Morning Star Mama. She had adapted to doing the women's chores in the camp. She learned to dance with the others. The girl was happy to have food cooked. She had learned to eat raw meat and berries to survive with mother wolf. Her Papa didn't cook any more, they guessed he just died and she was alone. She had to adapt to the wolf mother and follow her. Eventually she would tell what happened to her, but for now she was just happy to be with Mama Star and Silver Wing.

Swift Eagle went to the Dusty Road Trading Post for supplies. He was careful not to mention the white girl or her being at the camp. The braves knew not to talk about it and to stay away from her. Swift Eagle talked with the black smith Quint, he told him the Army was hanging Indians they caught who had taken vengeance on the white man. He told Swift Eagle he should bring his metal weapons to him and let him melt them. Swift Eagle came to Morning Star and told her he would be gone hunting some days and not to worry he had to do something.

He had enough supplies to last a week. He disappeared into the forest, going from tree to tree where he had caught the renegades and rendered justice to them, he gathered up the metal staves, then returned to the black smith Quinton's shop, and gave him the weapons Quinton threw them into the melting pot. No evidence was left to connect these bones to him should any one ever come across them. The renegades would never rape or kill their women and destroy their camp again.

Swift Eagle knew should the buffalo hunters or trappers try to harm any of the women in his camp there would be more skeleton bones in the woods, without the stave. He could mete them his kind of justice, knowing the stone stave worked just as well.

Red Beard was surprised when the pony express gave him a letter. Red Beard was surprised since he had no kin folks in this country. When he looked closely he could see it was from Brad Winthrop. He knew it was information for Swift Eagle. He opened the letter and read, Brad was on the way with material to build the house he promised for Morning Star. He had the deed recorded with his name on it but it would be her home. Red Beard could see it would take at least three months for the wagons to be here. He sent the Indian runner to Swift Eagles camp.

Swift Eagle came to the trading post and waited until he could listen in privacy to the letter his Uncle Brad Winthrop had written. Red Beard went to the kitchen and shut the door, he could read it without the other braves listening. Of course, they were anxious knowing Swift Eagle now had food and didn't have to trade furs for it. They knew it had something to do with Swift Eagle's white father and the uncle from Boston.

"What this mean house in wagon?"

"Well, yes sort of, Swift Eagle, it will be many moons until wagons are here. Uncle Brad Winthrop wants you to know."

"Aie, why Uncle Brad Winthrop write. Swift Eagle?"

"Yes, it is why. To let you know he not forget he promise you house for Morning Star."

They went back to the grocery room. Swift Eagle asked for dried apples and sugar. They now could have something besides hog fat and dried beans. The apples were delicious cooked slowly over the fire. It was a real treat for the four of them along with the venison stew and corn patty cakes.

The others knew the white girl was in their camp but didn't ask about her. They noticed Morning Star had colored her hair and darkened her face mainly so any white men coming by wouldn't notice her. She was now taking her place and doing chores Silver Wing did. Morning Star knew when Uncle Brad Winthrop came and read the Bible book, he would know who she was and if she had other people somewhere. She knew it best to keep her out of sight of the fur traders and buffalo hunter. Even Red Beard didn't know about her, the braves knew not to talk about her to anyone especially at the trading post. The camp was in the forest far enough to discourage anyone coming there and especially after what happened to the renegades who destroyed the camp. Word got around and they shied away from there.

Brad had told Swift Eagle to cut logs for the log house. Red Beard showed where the cabin house would be built. Swift Eagle had been chopping the logs and laying them where the house was going to be built. If Uncle Brad Winthrop was coming back with the wagon, window door, and stove like Red Beard said. Now he was happy to chop more logs. The other braves knew the promise the Uncle made to him. The parcel of ground Brad had purchased from the Scotsman was two miles from the trading post and the trees were thick between it and the store. Brad wanted his sister-in- law to have privacy in her new log cabin home. He hoped the girl would learn to read and write when he got there with a teacher. He even thought it would be good if there were a school just for the Indian children. With out reading or writing they didn't have a chance to advance in their life time. Some over-zealous religions wanted to take their heritage away from them. After all, Brad thought, they were here first this is really the Indians land, not the white man. Brad knew the world was changing, but the West was untamed. George Armstrong Custer had been put in his place by Chief Sitting Bull.

Brad knew he was not popular with Colonel Wesley because of his association with his brother's squaw wife, her son, and daughter. He felt the prejudices the Indians faced from just such ignorant white people. Of course when they found the wealth of Morning Star and her children, their attitude would change.

Strong Bow knew of White Cloud as he was courting Silver Wing. He was chopping trees and gathering rocks as Uncle Brad Winthrop told them to pile them up for a fire place in Morning Star's house

White Cloud had learned to talk now and could respond to the others, she stayed to herself though in her Star mama teepee. She called Morning Star Mama Star. Swift Eagle knew the braves were casting glances at White Cloud, but wanted Uncle Brad Winthrop to read White Cloud's name, she not Indian like Silver Wing.

The day finally came when the wagon rolled into the Dusty Trail Trading Post. Red Beard had been told it passed Fort McKinley, and was on their way. He sent a runner to the

61

camp to find Swift Eagle. As it happened, he and Strong Bow were out hunting. Uncle Brad Winthrop would have to wait. Brad and Ned, the man he hired to help drive the wagon, drove to the cleared site. They built a fire and cooked their supper over the coals. Brad had learned how to survive in the wilderness so to speak. They had beans and fried sow belly. Brad made some corn patties and baked them over the coals in an iron fry pan with a cover. He and Ned sat back against the wagon wheel eating and resting. They would sleep under the wagon as they had on the long trip here.

Morning came they had left over fried sow belly, corn pone, and black coffee. They began unloading the things from the wagon. By the end of the day Brad and Ned had the logs in place to start on the cabin. There would be one large room the fireplace on the end. The iron stove could sit by the fire place. But that would come later.

The morning found Swift Eagle and Strong Bow looking at the two men eating breakfast.

"Aiee aiee, Uncle Brad Winthrop, you now here?" Swift Eagle shouted.

Brad was surprised. He got up, went to Swift Eagle, put his arm on his shoulder, and shook his hand.

"Yes, I am now here. Who is this with you?" He was looking at the brave with Swift Eagle.

The brave answered himself. "Me. Strong Bow." He reached toward Brad and quickly grasped his hand and shook it. Seeing he was copying his friend. They were learning something new in greeting others.

"We have coffee and something to eat come, eat with us. This is, Ned. He helps build the cabin, drove wagon for me," Brad thought, *Here, I have started talking as my nephew does again.*

11

Actually, I like the way my relatives live and talk. At least they are honest and not trying to be something they aren't. The four of them sat drinking coffee and talking about the trip. How they had encounter bear on the way and Ned shot the bear to save the mules from being killed. They had rain and the wagon stuck, making them have to unload the wagon get it out of the bog hole, then load everything back again. It took several days to get on the trail again.

Swift Eagle told his uncle about finding the white girl and the Bible mama no hurt had with the writing they could not read to see what it say about White Cloud.

Swift Eagle and Strong Bow had coffee then went to their camp as they had been away now four days and wanted to take the venison to their camp.

"Bring the Bible book when you come back, Swift Eagle."

The braves disappeared in the forest toward their camp with the deer hung over their shoulder. Ned and Brad continued through the day placing the logs on top of each other, cutting notched to join the logs, and make them sturdy.

Strong Bow and Swift Eagle returned at dusk. They had four squirrel with them cleaned and ready to roast over the fire. After eating, they took their blankets, covered themselves, and slept for the night beside the flickering camp fire.

Brad thought his friends at the Boston Men's Club would be hard pressed to believe it if they saw him now in denim pants, covered in a blanket, sleeping on the ground around a camp fire with two Indian braves and his hired man. Well, he thought he enjoyed this more than a tux. And the stuffed shirts he had associated with in order to bring more business to his father's shipyard.

The men were awakened with the scream and snarl of a mountain lion. It had come up to the fire. Swift Eagle threw his knife as it bent over Uncle Brad Winthrop, it fell on him. He waked up startled, it fell on the man who jumped up, scrambling across the coals to the other side, half-awake wondering what happened. By them they all were watching the lion trying to bite the knife and get it out of its neck. Strong Bow had the lion by its throat, finished it off, and retrieved the knife, throwing it to Swift Eagle. Ned and Brad looked on speechless. They had encountered the bear and wild things on their trek here but this was an all together different incident. Brad put the coffee pot on the coals with water and coffee. He was awake now and shaking after finding out what happened.

When he first had the Bible, he opened it finding these were Swedish people. Greta and Niles Swenson. The little girl was named Megan, her birth recorded in hand written scrawl. There went on notes of the hardships, how the wolf had been found in the baby cradle snuggled up to her with a protecting paw over the baby she had pulled to her teats. When they tried to take the baby, the wolf snarled and pulled it closer until Greta realized this she wolf had lost her cubs and hearing the baby cries had adopted the baby girl as her own. Greta would wait until the she wolf would leave the cradle, then take the child nurse her, and place her back in the cradle. Niles had tried to get the wagon repaired, but to no avail finally resigned to staying and making the best of it there. Megan was five when her mother passed on. Niles buried her and it was then she saw him read the Bible over the grave and began calling it Bible mama no hurt.

Brad guessed her father had told the child her mother would not hurt any more as he had finished reading over her grave. He cooked and hunted through the years ahead not finding a way out while the child grew and became more like the wild animal than her father. She had watched him cook the food and learned to do this. She survived in the wilderness with out any help but the mother wolf. She stole food and the buckskin dress from Silver Wing, yet Swift Eagle hadn't caught her. Now she was one of their family. Brad could write the people they would have met in Texas but by this time it was doubtful they would be there. He would write and let the Pony Express take it when they came by the Dusty Road Trading Post next time. Red Beard held the letters if there were any. Usually it was a trapper or hunter writing home. The soldiers sent their mail from the fort. They always had a fresh horse for the pony express rider, he would leave the bag of mail, catch up the next bag, eat a bite of food, and be on his way again unless there was another rider waiting to go on with the mail pouch.

The colonel's wife was living at the fort now and the men had made an addition to the fort for their wives.

12

Brad stopped briefly when they passed the fort, seeing they had women there now. He thought perhaps his mother and father would want to come and meet their grand children on his next trip home and back. They could ride the stage coach it wouldn't take as long as trudging along with the mules and wagon. There was places along the path where the women could freshen up have something to eat and even stay over-night should they wish to. Well he would see about it in the future. He knew his mother would like to have her grand-children be educated. Brad knew too they would take the girl Megan under their wing to aquaint her to the white mans world, by now he wasn't sure if the girl would want to change. It took another month to complete the log cabin, there were three sections in the cabin a large room for the cooking, eating, and living quarters. The other sections would be private for sleeping area. Swift Eagle would have his place, as Morning Star hers, and the girls could share one space.

They men cut fire wood and stacked it out by the door. They built a fire in the fire place. Swift Eagle went to get his family and bring them to their new home. Swift Eagle would not however remove his teepee home. He would keep both homes, he thought he would sleep in his teepee at night and hunt at dawn and dusk for fresh meat for his family.

The others of the tribe watched Swift Eagle, his mother, sister, and followed him to the Dusty Road Trading Post. The pathway back of the store was narrow and about two miles to the log cabin Brad and Ned along with Swift Eagle and Strong bow had built for Morning Star, Silver Wing, and White Cloud. They had their things in the corner. Swift Eagle brought food from the Trading Post to the cabin. There were shelves near the iron cook stove and on the walls seperated the rooms

The girls shared a shelf with their things putting the moccasins under the shelf on the ground floor. Brad wanted to have wood for the floor but would bring the planks at another time. He had however packed some heavy cotton mattresses as he knew they slept on moss or leaves covered with fur or blankets, it would be better with the cotton mattress.

Morning Star lay her blanket over the one in her room. Swift Eagle had a fire in the fireplace. Brad had a special iron spit made to hang the meat or pots from over the fire. They were sturdy. He had one box packed with some dishes his mother wanted to send her daughter-in-law, spoons, forks, and long handled spoons to stir her stew pot.

Mrs. Winthrop couldn't imagine living as this woman did, but yet knew this was their way of life for what other could they have done with the white man crowding them out and pushing them further from what actually was their land to begin with. She would like to visit one day in the future and meet her daughter-in-law and her grandchildren. Brad gave her an idea of them and how they favored their white father. She had no regrets if her son Frank had been happy. He lived as he wanted and died fighting for what he believed in, his wife, family and his living. When he caught the renegades stealing his furs. Frank knocked him to the ground and was recovering his furs when the thief came up behind Frank, stabbed him in the back, slit his throat, grabbed the furs leaving him bleeding to death, and sneaked off into the forest. When the braves found Frank, he lived long enough to tell them what had happened, what the man looked like, and his name. The braves carried him to the camp where he died.

Swift Eagle vowed to avenge his father's death and did find the man still trying to steal the Indians furs. He fixed him so he could never do anyone harm again. Quint told him the Army would be looking for the renegade and the weapon he was killed with. Swift Eagle quickly retrieved them and Quint threw them in the melting pot. His knife was one all men carried.

Swift Eagle could hit a rabbit beside the head as quickly as with his arrow and have meat on the coals in no time. Some of the men coming west carried revolvers, though when hunting for a game at the poker table in a saloon. They never tarried around an Indian camp the only place for them was a dance hall and bar room.

Morning Star and Swift Eagle gave the Tall Brave Man Frank a sacred Indian burial. Their life went on as usual. Brad heard about the way his brother died, thought on it for a while, and decided Frank had chosen this life because he was happy here. Brad could understand. There was no greed except the white man's greed. He didn't have to answer to anyone if he went to church or not, if he wore a suit to work or just went in his buckskins. Brad wouldn't be satisfied to live this way without his other friends but he and Frank always differed in their ways and thoughts.

Brad told Swift Eagle he was going to come back with the Indian teacher and a white woman teacher to see if his sister and Megan would like to take the schooling. He would make arrangements at the fort to have a classroom for them and quarters for the teachers. He knew the Colonel's attitude toward the Indian. He didn't see how Colonel Wesley would know the male teacher was Indian. He dressed, spoke as a well-educated college graduate, which is what he was. It would be interesting to watch, but Brad wouldn't say anything except this man was a graduate from Cambridge University. He had been teaching school in England before coming to the United States. Brad had met him at the Boston Men's Club.

Before he left he talked with Morning Star, Silver Wing, and White Cloud, he wanted Swift Eagle with him as they discussed the teacher and what was to be.

Brad and Ned bid them farewell the next day. The Wells Fargo Stage coach came, the driver and man riding shot gun left the tired horses in the corral and hitched up fresh horses stopping long enough for fresh water, then off toward the fort and the next relay station to change the team of horses again for the long trek to where the train rails had come from Boston. At least this would go quicker than dragging over the rough trail in the wagon.

He knew the white girl might wish to go back to the ways of the white people. Brad's mother would welcome her as a daughter if she wished. Well time would tell and now they would have to wait and see. His mother would be delighted to have her. She was like the Indians who raised her and doubt she would change.

The Winthrop's, Mary Elizabeth and Frank Bradley, were happy to see their son return. The stage coach stopped where the rails ended. The rails would soon be all the way to Fort McKinley.

13

Ned, his carpenter and wagon driver went by buggy to his home. While Brad walked to his parent's house. They were delighted to see him and had many questions about their grandson, his mother, and sister. He first had a long hot bath, then dressed casually, and went to the front porch to join them there. They wished to hear all about the cabin, their daughter-in-law, and grandchildren.

He leaned back in the porch swing, sipping a glass of iced lemonade, put his feet up, and started the story from the beginning.

Brad told them their grandchildren were handsome and favored the Winthrop's. They were very intelligent, just uneducated. The daughter-in-law was petite for an Indian and had fine features. He could see how his brother, Frank, would have fallen in love with her. She was unspoiled not like the girls he had dated in college.

They then wanted to know how their son had died. Brad told the story of the renegade he caught stealing his furs, had knocked the culprit to the ground, and to turned pick up his furs when the renegade thief, attacked, stabbing him in the back, and cutting his throat. The braves from the camp found Frank and he died in the camp telling them the name of the man who attacked him. Then how their grandson, Swift Eagle tracked the renegade who murdered his father. Swift Eagle caught him, and rendered his own justice for killing his father. Mary Elizabeth looked at her son, Brad in disbelief and said, "You means our grandson killed the man?"

"Yes, Mother, I mean Swift Eagle, your grandson, killed the man who killed his father."

"Oh my goodness wasn't there any law to arrest this man?"

"No, there isn't, Mother. The law doesn't care about the Indians and Frank was considered an Indian by the government. They looked the other way but Frank's son rendered the only kind of law the renegade would understand, it settled the score. Other trappers and buffalo hunters knew better than try to steal the Indians furs or destroy their home and camp."

"I hate to know my son was killed this way. I know he wrote that he loved his wife and would live there with her people."

"Yes, Elizabeth, he did what he wanted to do, try to understand dear," her husband told her. She was wiping tears and crying silently.

Brad then said, "Mother, you would be delighted to meet your grandchildren and see Frank left you two fine grandchildren."

They sat in silence, the afternoon sun was going down and the crickets started their song for the evening.

Martha, the house keeper, came to the front door. "Miss Mary, dinner is served."

They went in to have dinner and finish Brad's first day home. He was glad to sleep on his bed with a spring under him for the first time in over a year now. Mary Elizabeth still mourned the death of her son Frank. Her husband knew she would have to get over it. There wasn't anything he could say to comfort her. He, too, was hurt but tried to hide it from her.

Brad told them there was a white girl with them and he would tell them about her and how she survived in the wild untill Swift Eagle captured her.

"Really, Brad, she was captured by our grandson?"

They, of course, were anxious to find out why a white girl would be living with an Indian tribe unless she was a captive. Brad assured them she was not a captive.

"I will explain in the morning, Father." He hurried off to bed before they could ask any more questions.

• • • • •

The next morning Brad enjoyed breakfast with his parents. Martha had ham, fresh baked biscuits, home churned butter, scrambled eggs, fresh sliced tomatoes, and hot coffee to wash it down with.

Brad would meet with the two people who had answered the ad in the local paper wishing to go see the west and teach there in a school. Brad wondered if they really knew what they would be getting into. He would explain so they wouldn't be expecting more than what there was. He knew also, his mother and father wanted to go with them to meet their grandchildren. Well, it was a great deal different than what mother lived with here.

Brad met with Julie Rawls, a petite blonde, blue eyed, tiny, vivacious young woman in her late thirties ready to tackle the wilderness. She knew it would be a challenge yet interesting, whose parents didn't want her to leave Boston and Randy

Swain was muscular, tall, bronze skinned, black haired man with piercing brown eyes. He was quiet, well-mannered, yet aware of everything around him.

The teachers who planned to go with him when he returned to finish seeing to his brother's children and their future. He explained to them the hardships they would encounter and wanted them to know up front. He was waiting for a letter from the Colonel at Fort McKinley informing him quarters had been built for a school room and living quarters for the two teachers, plus a room for his parents at the fort. They would return though after meeting their grandchildren. They didn't intend to stay in the wilderness, their home was here in Boston. Mary Elizabeth would find this quite different than the Ladies Bridge Club.

Brad told them it would be best not to mention Randy was an Indian. The soldiers had a dim view of them and he was sure they couldn't understand an Indian college graduate. Brad had been home a year when the letter came from the Colonel at Fort McKinley. The school was ready for students and the living quarters were completed. They could come as soon as possible. Well, Brad thought, *It's fine, Colonel, but we will wait before starting and avoid the winter weather on the road.* He booked passage on the stage coach for them. Spring came and they were waiting to board when the coach pulled into the station.

The four sat inside and Brad joined the driver and shot gun guard on the top. They would lay over the first night. It would take some time before getting to the fort. He knew his mother would be weary and glad to rest a few days before going to the Dusty Road Trading Post to meet her grandchildren.

Brad told his mother it would take at least three if not four months by stage coach to get there. He wanted her to know there could be break downs along the way and they would layover at relay stations. It would be uncomfortable for her. She was determined. If she had grandchildren from Frank, she would endure the hardships to meet them.

14

The five boarded the Stage Coach headed for Tennessee, Brad rode on top with the driver and shot gun guard, the luggage was on the rear, covered with canvas. The first few days were not too tiresome, but the next days the passengers began to feel the strain.

Frank Bradley and Randy Swain got out and walked around when they stopped at a relay station, the ladies didn't go too far from the station. They found the outdoor privy. It was a relief from finding bushes to hide behind to relieve themselves. Brad explained all of this to his parents and the teachers. They didn't complain realizing it was what they had been told in advance.

After two months they reached the Fort. Mary Elizabeth and Julie breathed a sigh of relief. The soldiers escorted them to their living quarters. Brad had stored cotton mattresses for them on the coach and the soldiers put them on their bunks in the rooms prepared for them. Brad went to the soldiers' bunkroom where he had stayed before. Randy and Julie had their individual rooms close to the school room. Frank and Mary Elizabeth had a room on the other side of theirs. Mary Elizabeth was glad to find the mattress of cotton to lay on. She washed up in the basin and went with the others to the officer's mess. They had venison, fried and mashed potatoes with gravy, and biscuits. Mary Elizabeth knew her son had warned her of the inconvenience and she vowed to herself to say nothing about it. She most graciously thanked the colonel for his hospitality. After dinner she washed the dust off, then to rest and sleep for a day before coming out of their room. The Colonel couldn't believe this society woman would want an Indian grandson much less come to meet him.

Brad wondered if the rural town of Black Water would have had a hotel or perhaps something better for his parents to stay at while they were here. Well, he would see how things were when she was rested

The runner came and told them at the Trading Post Swift Eagle's grandmother and grandfather were at the fort and his Uncle Brad. Two teachers came with him. Swift Eagle wanted to see what his Tall Man Brave Frank's mother and his father looked like. He knew his Uncle Brad Winthrop would come there as soon as he could. It was a long ride to come here and they were tired.

He remembered his father showing them about letters and talking about teachers who told him of the letters and numbers. He wondered if this is what Uncle Brad Winthrop had with him at the fort. He called them teachers like his father, Frank, told them about.

Well, today he had other things to do. They needed fresh meat and he was going hunting. It was good to have the food at Dusty Road Trading Post, but it was salted pork which was good. Yet he and his mother liked the fresh deer meat to cook with the potatoes and onions from the trading store. Now that he had wampum it was easy to just hunt for fresh meat. He disappeared into the forest behind the camp grounds. Silver Wing and White Cloud watched him leave, they decided to go and pick berries, so their mother could cook with sugar and make flour dumplings.

Morning Star was busy straightening the blankets and put the dishes away in the teepee. She knew that Frank's brother would be disappointed she moved back to her teepee. She wasn't happy living in the cabin with the children, the buffalo hunters, and trappers had found them alone and were constantly taunting them. Morning Star didn't want Swift Eagle to know and do something about it. It wouldn't stop the ignorant white men and she was concerned about her two daughters now being there alone without others of her tribe. Morning Star thought it would be good if the cabin could be moved on their camp ground and they could all share the storage space of it. She would ask her brother-in-law Brad Winthrop when he came to see the children.

Morning Star remembered how her Tall Brave Man Frank told her how the white men in the government didn't treat the true Americans as they should. They were here originally and the Great Thunder Bird had left them in this land to be free. When the white people came in their sailing vessels and landed he told her the Indians helped them survive through the winter when it was so cold. The Indians taught them how to plant and fertilize their seed with the fish they caught from rivers and ocean.

As they could see the renegades and buffalo hunters ruined it for both the Indians and the white settlers who tried to live in peace in the new country. Now she had to move to her teepee to keep her and her daughters safe with her people. She wondered about her children going to learn the white way of writing and numbers. Her Frank told her before he died they would need this kind of learning.

• • • • •

In the meantime, Swift Eagle decided to wait by the quick sand pond for the animals to come and drink. He thought it would be best hunting there. He lay by the bushes on the other side of the pond. He was thinking of his father and how he wanted him and Silver Wing to learn to read and write with a stick like Red Beard did. He couldn't believe what he saw and was hearing. There in front of him stood his father, Tall Brave Man Frank.

"Father, Father, I thought you were dead I am so happy to see you. How did you get here?"

"Swift Eagle my son I am with your ancestors in the spirit world. I wanted to come talk with you here alone and let you see me."

"Oh, yes, Father, it is good I see you now. I happy."

"Son, you listen while I have talk with you not much time I am here in spirit."

"Yes, father, me listen."

"You do as Uncle Brad tells you. I know it will be hard for you and your sister to learn the white mans talk and the ways they do things. Do you hear what I say?"

"Yes, Father, I hear what you say."

"If you are to live any kind of life and help your mother, you will need to learn to write with the stick called a pencil. You will need to learn the numbers to count you wampum, the white man calls it money. Do you understand what I say?"

"Yes, Father, I will hear what brother Uncle Brad tell me to do. I want to help mother and care for her now you not with her."

"Yes, Son, I knew you would understand I cannot stay any longer." His voice dwindled off to a whisper, and his father sort of vaporized into the mist in the forest.

Swift Eagle stood up looking slowly around. At the pond, was a buck deer drinking, he raised his bow and shot the animal. Quickly he skinned and cleaned it, then returned to the camp with the fresh venison for his mother, and enough to share with the others. Morning Star heard him coming through the forest. She and the girls waited to see what he had for their dinner tonight.

"Mother, here is fresh meat for us and others in camp who are without meat,"

She quickly cut the meat and divided it with the others in their camp at their fires. She boiled the meat in the iron pot Brad brought to the cabin from Boson. It hung from the iron frame he had for the fireplace. Here it hung over the open fire. Swift Eagle came and spoke to her.

"Mother, I know you will think I was asleep and when I tell you this."

"What you mean, Swift Eagle?" she stirred the stew with the long handled spoon, then turned and looked over at him sitting by their teepee.

"Tall Brave Man Frank, my father, came to see me today when me hunt at quick sand pond. Me wait for deer to come drink water."

"Were you sleeping Swift Eagle?"

"No, Mother, me see father, others with him. Ancestors he say."

She stopped stirring the pot of boiling stew meat. She looked over at him.

"Did father say? What he want, Swift Eagle?"

"Yes, he say what he want me to do. So now you believe me not sleeping?"

"Yes, me believe, Swift Eagle, not sleeping when he see father."

"Father want me and Silver Wing to learn what Uncle Brad Winthrop wishes. Is why he come in spirit with ancestors."

"Oh, yes, now Morning Star understand why my husband come to see you."

"My father not stay long. Him go soon. Me happy me see Tall Brave Man, father."

"You listen to Uncle Brad he smart man, too like Tall Brave Man Father.

"I will do what Uncle Brad Winthrop say."

"Yes, Son, I will listen and learn how to use the stick they write with. I will learn to read if I can go to hear teacher too."

"Mother, I will hope you do learn with me and sisters, White Cloud and Silver Wing. We learn together."

She filled their bows with the delicious venison stew. They sat around the fire in the evening eating and enjoying each other being together. The others of the tribe had shared the deer meat Swift Eagle had hunted in the morning. Swift Eagle fixed his blanket back of the Teepee as he had been sleeping out there to be sure the others were protected and gave them privacy, he had a small teepee for him in case of rain he could hurry inside. He knew also Uncle Brad Winthrop would be sad because Morning Star and his sisters were not staying at the log cabin he had built for them. He knew his Uncle would understand when he found the white rough necks had been taunting his mother. She was not going to stay there and have any more trouble. She knew her son would catch these men and take vengeance on them. She and the girls silently moved back to the camp and put up their Teepee. She was happy to be there with the others anyway. Strong Bow was courting Silver Wing he was disheartened, when he found she would be leaving to go to what was called school to learn to write and to read as the white man did. He didn't want to lose Silver Wing to anyone she was to be his squaw and he loved her. Silver Wing was looking forward to learning to read story White Cloud had told her how her Bible mama would read to her and her papa every night. It was good to hear her mama read the Bible story about David and a giant man. Silver Wing wondered why White Cloud hadn't learned to read the Bible. Silver Wing didn't understand White Cloud was too young yet to read when her mama died. She could only remember the mama reading it. White Cloud could recall more of her papa until the wolf mother had adopted her as one of her cubs when Papa died she was with wolf mother, all the time then. She did remember sneaking to their camp and stealing food and watching them. White Cloud wanted to learn to read too and to use the stick to write.

It would be good to use the pencil and to read the Bible. Uncle Brad Winthrop told Swift Eagle, he could read many books about little boys who lived on a boat on the river. He wondered about the little boy. Why did he live on a river? Well he would learn to read like the white man did and Red Beard at the Trading Post. He wrapped in his blanket and fell asleep back in his mother's teepee. The night was cool and he could hear the hoot owls calling to each other, then a lone wolf howling in the distance, he soon feel asleep.

15

Meantime at the fort, Brad was sleeping in the soldiers bunk room with them. He lay there thinking he had heard of the rural town of Black Water, and they did have an old one room school house, a hotel, saloon, black smith, a stable, and even a country store. He thought it would be more convenient if his mother and dad had a room at the hotel, at least they had baths there. He decided to take a look at this rural town of Black Water and see what it was like. He thought he would ask Randy Rawls to go with him and see how he thought about the school. There might be other children who wished to attend school but didn't have a teacher and here they had two teachers. Brad would talk to teacher Rawls in the morning. He soon drifted to sleep, dreamed of bears attracting his buggy, awakened in a sweat then drifted off again. The bugler blowing his wake up call awakened him and the others before day light, he washed, shaved dressed, and hurried to the soldier's mess hall. The breakfast was the usual fresh hot biscuits, fried sow belly, and scorch gravy, topped off with hot biscuits, delicious blueberry jam, and hot coffee. Really it was quite good. Brad wondered how his mother would fare after not having scrambled eggs, fried bacon, and marmalade to go with her toast and coffee. Of course, there wasn't any butter in the fort. Forget it. He had warned his mother and he would be interested to see what she would say about the food here at the fort. After breakfast he went to his mother and dad's room. They were ready to go out to the parade grounds and fresh air.

"Oh, there you are, Brad. I must say I was glad to find a mattress to finally get a good night's sleep on, after the time on the trail in the Wells Fargo coach and the way stations. "

"Really, Mother, I am glad to hear you rested, how about you father, did you sleep well?"

"Yes, Son I did, and I am anxious to rent or acquire a horse and buggy as soon as we can to go meet our grandchildren."

About this time Randy came out and joined them.

"Good morning."

"Hello, Randy." They continued walking to the parade ground outside.

"Mother, there is a bench over a way if you'd like to sit a while here."

"Yes, Son, I see it. I will go over there and enjoy the fresh morning air"."

"I wanted to talk with Dad and Randy this morning. I will be there in a few minutes, Mother." The men walked to the far wall of the fort, and while they walked Brad told them of the school and hotel in Black Water, asking if they would accompany him there to see what it was like. Also, to see if they would rather stay there and have school and room at the hotel where it would be more convenient and comfortable, they hoped.

"Yes, Brad, I would like to. I know you mother would be happy if there was a church I wouldn't mind a drink at the saloon, if it's not wild like the western stories I've read about."

Brad smiled and looked down. Randy just stood by quietly. He cleared his throat and said nothing. Randy knew how these saloons are in the rural cow towns and it was to his way of thinking Brad's father would be out of place in the saloon. He would go with them and see how the town was. He didn't want any trouble from the whites in the town because of the students being half breeds and himself being an educated Indian. If it seemed like it would be better to remain at the fort, he would. What he didn't know was Quint, the black smith, was also Indian and friend of Swift Eagle. Quint had made the weapons for Swift Eagle.

Brad asked the Colonel if he could use the horse and buggy to take his parents to Dusty Road Trading Post.

"Yes, Mr. Winthrop, you are welcome to use it. I would suggest you have my soldiers contact Red Beard so you could like to meet with your nephew before you travel all that way. You really need protection from the bears in the wooded area."

"You are correct, Sir, I hadn't given it enough thought. Thank you, Sir, I appreciate you asking them to do just so when we go."

"They will go today and return. I wouldn't be surprised to see your half-breed nephew return to guide you and his grandparents to the trading post."

Brad thought, *What an ignorant bastard this man is.* "I will be waiting to hear from them, Sir." Brad walked over to the bench with the others and told them what was going on.

"Oh, well then, perhaps my grandson will come to see us here first, Brad."

"Well we will wait and see. The Colonel said the soldiers would tell the runner at the trading post. He will run to the camp and tell Swift Eagle we are here."

"My, it's so strange to hear you call my grandson by his Indian name."

"I would guess the Indians use the names they think the best for their children's skills. They don't have all the names like Mary, John, David, and such. I guess, Mother, it's why they use those names."

"I will get used to it, Brad." She was enjoying the fresh morning air coming in through the open gates of the fort. It certainly was different from her home in Boston.

Before they returned to their room, they watched the two soldiers leave for the Dusty Road Trading Post. It would be late afternoon before they returned. Mrs Winthrop took advantage of the afternoon and rested before dinner. The men walked around the fort, then sat waiting for dinner on the bench by the parade grounds.

It was almost dark when the soldiers returned. To Brad's surprise Swift Eagle was with them. He rode behind one of the soldiers. He jumped down, hurried to the front of the fort, and asked to see his Uncle Brad Winthrop. The soldier on duty went to the mess hall where Brad was just finished eating dinner. He was surprised and hurried to greet his nephew.

In the meantime, Colonel Wesley ambled to the front of the fort being curious to see what this white man's half-breed nephew looked like. Quite to his surprise, the man waiting there looked a great deal like his uncle. He was dressed neatly in his buckskins and moccasins, his hair was neatly pulled back, and tied in back of his head.

Brad rushed forward and took him by the shoulder, shaking his hand. Swift Eagle was quite surprised at his greeting.

"Hello, Swift Eagle, it's good seeing you again. It's been over a year now, how is your mother and your sister, Silver Wing?"

Swift Eagle, looked at the colonel standing there. Why was he there, was something wrong?

"Morning Star good sister, Silver Wing good, Uncle Brad Winthrop" He answered still wondering why the colonel was standing there.

Brad caught the reason his nephew was puzzled. Brad turned to the colonel and said, "Oh, yes, Colonel, I would like you to meet my nephew, Swift Eagle, he is here to meet his grandparents from Boston."

This time Colonel Wesley was taken by surprise as Swift Eagle reached out to shake hands with the man.

"Me pleased to meet you, Colonel."

Brad was surprised at his nephew. He had picked up quite a lot from the white people in his greeting to the Colonel.

"Harrumph, uh, well yes, Swift Eagle, I am pleased to meet you also," the colonel finally reached out and shook hands with the brave. Coughing, and clearing his throat, he walked quickly past them on to the parade grounds, shaking his head, and muttering to himself. Brad was secretly amused, *Well, this ole man didn't realize his nephew knew how to shake hands.* Brad was pleased with Swift Eagle.

"Come in, Swift Eagle, let us go to the vacant room they built just in case they wished to start a school room here. I will go get you grandparents to come meet you."

They went to the opposite end of the fort from where they were. There were six rows of benches lined up against the wall, a blackboard, and a desk in the front with a chair back on it in case there was a meeting and the chairman could sit there.

"I will be right back, Swift Eagle." He hurried to his parents' room.

"Mother, Father, your grandson is here. Come with me he is waiting in the school room."

Mary Elizabeth quickly brushed her hair back from her face, looked over at her husband, then they joined Brad in the hall and hurried to the school room to meet their grandson, Frank's only son. As they came to the door, Brad opened it and stepped into the room. He looked at his nephew standing tall by the front desk looking toward them. He could see his brother Frank as he stood there waiting. Brad went over to Swift Eagle and said, "Mother, Father, come and meet your grandson, Swift Eagle, this is Franks son."

"Oh my, he looks just like his father." she said tears in her eyes.

"Yes, dear, he does favor our son Frank."

Swift Eagle looked at the tiny woman and tall man standing there in the door. They were his father's mother and father, his grandmother and grandfather. He walked slowly toward them as they stood looking at him. He reached out to his grandfather and said. "Hello, father of my father, Tall Brave Man Frank."

Mr. Bradley quickly grasp his grandson's hand and his shoulder with the other hand they stood face to face, each man a good six feet, six inches tall.

"I am happy to see you my grandson, Swift Eagle." He then turned to the woman by him and reached his hand to her.

"Hello, mother of my father, Tall Brave Man Frank I happy to see my grandmother, Mary."

She smiled and said, "I am happy to see you my grandson, you favor your father, my son Frank." She took his hand.

He thought she has such a little hand to have the tall sons. He thought his mother would like her husband's mother and father.

His mother, Morning Star, worked, her hands, and stature were larger than the petite grandmother Mary.

"Shall we go sit so we can talk?" she asked.

They walked to the benches and sat facing each other. Brad kept the conversation going about meeting his sister the next day and his mother, Morning Star, their daughter-in-law. Swift Eagle couldn't help looking at them and thinking these white people were his grandparents. They were blood related like his father was blood-brother to the tribe. After a while they decided it was time to return to their room and rest for the night.

Brad then said, "Swift Eagle, I will bring blankets and we will sleep by the wall at the gate tonight."

His mother was astonished at her son, but said nothing. They bid them good night and went to their room. Mary kept talking into the night. Her husband was snoring, not hearing a word she was saying about how much this young man was like her son, Frank.

Frank smiled and said, "Yes, Dear," and fell back to sleep as she talked on during the night. Finally, falling asleep near daylight.

Brad quickly gathered up two blankets and hurried back to meet his nephew at the bench out side.

They went to the wall near the two closed gate doors and bedded down for the night. Swift Eagle was surprised at his Uncle Brad Winthrop not staying in the fort, he had a blanket with him he planned to spend the night here and show the way the next morning and protect his new family also. He thought this was really strange seeing these people and knowing they were same blood.

Early next morning the bugler awakened them standing by the flag pole blowing time to get up. Brad and Swift Eagle hurried to the pump outside the fort to wash up Brad told Swift Eagle he would go shave and be back soon. He waited for him at the bench at the front of the fort. When he returned he had biscuits, fried sow belly and a large container of coffe with him, he had two cups. They sat there eating the biscuits and meat drinking the coffee black.

"Good food Uncle Brad Winthrop." He said.

"Yes the biscuits are different than the corn meal bread your mother Morning Star makes."

"Yes it is different. What we do today, Uncle Brad Winthrop.?"

"Well Swift Eagle for one thing will you just call me Uncle Brad?"

He went to put the cups and containers back then hurried to get the horse and buggy rigged up so they could start early and have more time with their family at the Dusty Road Trading Post. There was room enough in the buggy for the two men to ride near the front where the steps were. It was about a two hour ride to the Trading Post.

There was a group of Indian braves waiting near the hitching rack to see what Morning Star's family looked like. This was really something different for them. The only different people were the fur traders and those men who traded there. Morning Star and Silver Wing along with White Cloud were in the Trading Post waiting in the kitchen to meet them.

Brad helped his mother and father down from the buggy. Swift Eagle went ahead with Brad and his parent's walking behind them. They went into the store. Red Beard came around the counter and greeted them.

"Aye, there, Captain. Glad to meet ye, just call me Red Beard as the others do. I am a danged Scotsman, sort of lost out here in the wilderness."

Bradley reached out and said, "Well there, Red Beard, I am a Scotsman, too, but from Boston. Glad to make your acquaintance, Sir, and, meet my wife, Mrs. Winthrop."

She nodded to the Scotsman and waited to meet her daughter-in-law and granddaughter. She could hardly wait.

Swift Eagle then said, "Grandmother now meet my mother, Morning Star, and your granddaughter, Silver Wing." She followed him through the door into the small kitchen.

Mary went to the Indian woman, Morning Star stood up, they looked at each other a moment, Mary smiled and reached out taking her daughter-in-law in her arms saying, "I am so happy to meet you my Dear. Frank wrote me how lovely you were and how much he loved you. I have waited a long time to meet you." She backed away looking at the bewildered Morning Star, she never had affection shown to her like this. Mary quickly went to the girls and hugged Silver Wing then turned to the white girl.

"You will be my granddaughter, too, White Cloud." She hugged her also.

Frank stood inside the door watching them, smiling. As well as the puzzled expression on their faces at this emotion Mary Elizabeth had shown. He walked up to her and said, "Morning Star, I am you husband Frank's father. I am happy to meet Frank's wife." He then turned to the girls. "Young ladies, I am glad to see you and be your grandfather. Shall we sit down and visit or would you like to go outside and have a nice fresh drink of cold water. I am sort of thirsty from the dusty road."

Brad and Swift Eagle knew the other Indians wanted to look and watch how the white father and mother of Frank looked and talked. They were really curious to see if they were like their blood-brother Frank Tall Brave Man. They went to the sulphur flowing well, Mr. Bradley had ask Red Beard for a cup for Mary to drink from. He rinsed the cup, filled it, and handed it to Mary. He then leaned down cupped his hand and drank from the flowing well.

"Ah, it was good." He rose up wiping his face on his sleeve. Mary gave the cup back to him, by now they all had a refreshing drink from the flowing well. They decided to go where it was shady under some huge live oak trees. The girls and men sat on the ground. Mary still standing. "Aye, Mrs. Winthrop, I'll get ye a chair." The Scotsman hurried back, with a straight chair for Mary.

"Thank you, Mr. Red Beard." She sat by the others smiling down at them.

"This is lovely here in the shade under the trees, isn't it, Brad?" she asked her son.

Brad then replied, "Well, Morning Star, what do you think about your husband Frank's mother and father?" Brad said looking over at his sister-in-law.

Morning Star was quiet a moment then replied, "Brother of my husband, she is little woman to have tall brave sons."

Mary smiled when she heard what Morning Star said about her being little. She then replied, "Brad, I think my new daughter and two granddaughters are lovely."

Brad smiled, he guessed lovely meant she like them.

Morning Star then said, "Me like the mother of Tall Brave Man Frank, mother very lovely."

"Yes, Mary Elizabeth, our daughter and granddaughters are lovely I am so proud of them."

The girls laughed. They thought the word lovely must be good.

Mary wondered about the white girl. How would she be raised and would she stay with the Indians or what? She then thought, if they could learn to read and write she hoped it would give each of them a chance in life even though Frank had left money and holding to keep her daughter-in-law for her lifetime.

The braves from the camp sat away from them listening to their talking and their different features, the woman was so much smaller than their women, she had golden hair like

White Cloud, her nose and ears were small, too. They murmured to one another about this.

Brad then approached the subject about them moving to Black Water to attend school and asked if they knew anything about Black Water. Swift Eagle was alert when he heard his uncle mention Black Water.

"Me know Black Water, Uncle Brad."

"Tell us about Black Water, Swift Eagle."

"Me know Quint, he blacksmith, my friend."

"Do you know if there is a church in Black Water?"

"Me think is church in Black Water. We go see, Uncle Brad?"

Yes, Swift Eagle, I think we will go see what there is in Black Water. The soldiers in the fort tell me there is a hotel and at one time there was a school and it had a teacher and children but they moved away from Black Water and no one is left to teach at the school."

"Me see little braves play in road kick can no in school."

"We shall go and see what's in Black Water." Brad replied.

Brad would see if they could use the horse and rig. He went to the office and ask Colonel Wesley if he could rent the horse and rig for a trip to Black Water. The colonel didn't mind him using the rig, but he was curious why he wanted to go to Black Water. Brad explained to the colonel his mother was a church going woman and he had been told by the soldiers Black Water had a church, a saloon, a black smith, and even an old school building with a bell tower now vacant. It hadn't been in use for some time. The children were left without a teacher there.

"Oh, yes, well, now I can understand why you want to see Black Water. I haven't been there for some time either."

"Me has been there many times to see friend Quint, black smith."

"Then your nephew will be able to direct you to the town and also protect you as you travel the woods road through the forest between here and there. It's about ten miles from Dusty Road Trading Post."

"Thank you. We will start in the morning then, Colonel, if it's all right with you." He nodded and walked on to the open gates at the fort.

Brad wondered if his mother would mind staying here at the fort until the men returned from Black Water. He would ask Swift Eagle to ask his mother and his sisters, if they would stay here with his mother and Julie, until they returned. Actually, it would be good. They would have an opportunity to get better aquainted with each other. Of course, Julie and Mary did embroidery work and made quilts. They also had a game called checkers but hadn't brought it with them. Well he thought, *They would think of something to talk about.*

"I talk with mother and sisters, Uncle Brad."

Brad could see his nephew was learning more new words.

It would be a problem solved, if they would stay here at the fort. The ladies could have dinner served in the officer's mess. They wouldn't be in the main mess hall with the soldiers.

Swift Eagle went to his mother he ask her if they would stay at the fort with Mary Winthrop and Julie Rawls, the school teacher, until they returned from Black Water. Morning Star really didn't want to stay at the fort, but she knew Frank's mother and the school teacher would not sleep on the ground in her teepee either. It was best if they stay with them at the fort. She was used to the strange looks from the soldiers looking her and her daughter's dressed in buckskins, not clothes like the white people wore. Yes, she would stay until they returned she told her son.

Brad told his mother and Julie what they planned to do. At first his mother didn't want them to be alone there until she found Morning Star and her daughters would stay with them until they came back. He explained to them how her daughter-in-law would be gazed at by the soldiers because of their different way of dress. It was uncomfortable to Morning Star, yet she agreed to stay with her mother-in-law. The ladies were pleased. Morning Star and her daughters would sleep in the male teacher's room and go with the others to the officer's mess hall, and sit with them to eat their meals. Mary would try to keep her daughter-in-law at ease if possible.

The men slept outside leaving Randy Swain's room for Morning Star, Silver Wing, and White Cloud to share. The girls were used to curling in a blanket on the ground and left his bed to their mother.

The next morning before they left they accompanied the women to the officer's mess hall. The men stood as they entered the room and they were shown where to sit. The two girls looked around and sat down by their mother, the teacher, Julie, and Mary Winthrop. The men were invited to join them across the table. They were served the ordinary biscuits, scorch gravy, jam, and hot coffee. It was a treat for them. They hurriedly returned to their rooms after breakfast and then joined the men as they left the fort in the buggy. Frank and Randy sat on the seat, Brad and Swift Eagle sat down where the foot rest was while Frank held the reins. Brad had a gun this time. If a bear attacked the horse again, of course Swift Eagle had his bow, arrows, and knife. They waved and started down the woods road toward the rural town of Black Water. They had water with them and grain for the horse, enough to take them all the way to the town.

• • • • •

The morning air was refreshing and things went quite well along the road. They stopped briefly at the trading post, picked up some coffee, and condensed milk. It was afternoon when they came into town. Swift Eagle showed them to Quint's home and black smith shed. They tied the horse and stepped down to meet with Quint.

He immediately recognized Randy as a blood brother but never said anything. He held his hand to the men. "I am glad to meet you."

They shook hands and Brad then began to tell Quint why they were here. After being there a while and asking questions, Brad found they had the school house and it was vacant. There was a one room jail and the local sheriff. He thought they should talk to him about starting a school. They could look at the hotel and see if they thought Mary and the others would want to room or may be find a house for rent there. The men left the horse in Quint's corral with feed. There was plenty of grass for grazing and water.

They went first to the sheriff's building. It was one room shack with a room behind the sheriff's table with bars. The sheriff sat on the porch outside watching the men as they walked his way. He pushed his hat back and squinted to see them better.

They stopped in front of him and Brad said, "Hello, Sheriff Henry. I am Brad Winthrop, this is my father, Mr. Frank Winthrop, Mr. Randy Swain, and my nephew Indian brave, Swift Eagle Winthrop. We would like to talk with you if you have time.

Sheriff Henry leaned forward in his chair, "I am pleased to meet you fellers. Let's go over to the saloon where we can sit and talk."

They followed him down the road and across to Calhoun's. The place was empty, it smelled of tobacco smoke and stale beer. They sat at a table near the small dance floor, and an old upright piano. A man came from the back. He had a white apron tied around his waist.

"Hey, Sheriff, what's this? Do we have new neighbor in town?'

"Yes, Calhoun, this is Mr. Frank Winthrop, his son Brad Winthrop, Mr. Randy Swain, and Mr. Winthrop's grandson, Swift Eagle Winthrop."

The three men stood up to shake Calhoun's hand. Swift Eagle quickly stood and extended his hand. Calhoun looked over at the Sheriff, then quickly shook hands with the brave. He secretly wondered about this strange group of men and wondered about the man called Randy Swain. He was dressed as the others, but his skin was darker. He spoke very correctly, too.

"Would you fellows like a drink or something to eat?" Calhoun asked waiting there.

"What do you have to eat Calhoun?" Sheriff Henry asked.

"We have beans, biscuits, and some fried hog jowl."

Brad looked at Swift Eagle, "What would you like, Swift Eagle?"

"Uncle Brad, I want beans and biscuit."

Brad looked at Randy and his father, Randy looked over at Frank waiting politely for his response.

"Oh, yes, Mr. Calhoun, I would like the beans and biscuit, coffee ,too, please."

"I will have the same, Mr. Calhoun," Randy replied.

"Yes, Sir, I will have the same" Sheriff Henry said, leaning back looking up at Calhoun. "Calhoun, I thought you had steaks here in this place?"

"Sheriff, we have steaks on Saturday nights when the cowboys are here then we butcher a cow. I thought you knew."

"Well, I do now and I will have the same as these other fellers."

Randy looked at Sheriff Henry and asked, "Sheriff, when was the school last open for students?"

"Well, Mr. Swain, as near as I recollect, it's three years or maybe five since we had a school teacher. The last one moved with her family to New York leaving us without a teacher. Would you happen to be a teacher?" he looked over Randy puzzled.

"Yes, Sheriff, I am a college graduate, educated at University College, London, England."

"Oh, I see now why you folks is askin' about a hotel, the school and everything."

Mr. Winthrop then spoke up, "Yes, Sheriff, my wife is here with me at Fort McKinley. I wondered if the hotel here would be open this time of day."

"Well, it's usually open on Saturdays when the cowboys are in town."

"Sheriff, after we finish would you show us the hotel and perhaps introduce us to the owner?" Bradley Winthrop asked.

Calhoun went to the kitchen and came back with the bowls of beans and a platter of hot biscuits just baked, with a large container of wild berry jam. He returned again with a coffee pot and five cups. He placed the pot on the table to pour their own. Swift Eagle didn't waste any time, he poured his coffee added sugar, spread jam on the biscuit and forgot every other thing except his food. The others finished. Frank pulled his billfold out and asked Calhoun how much they owed. He paid the man while the others waited at the door.

The sheriff then showed them to the only hotel in town. It was at the very edge of town near the school house. It looked half way decent, Brad was thinking of his mother, but of course it wasn't the Broadwater Arms, in Boston. He thought he best see if it was a brothel instead of a hotel, for sure he wouldn't bring them into *that* kind of place. They walked on to the Shady Grove Hotel. It was a two story building, a wide porch with benches, ran completely around the building, the wide steps led to the front door, there were stairs on either side of the building. It looked as if there were twelve rooms. The men climbed the steps, Sheriff Henry, stood at the door and called out.

"Miss Daisy, Miss Daisy, you have customers out here." They heard foot steps coming along a hall way, the door opened, Miss Daisy came out on the porch. She was a small woman with gray hair who looked to be in her sixties.

"Hello, Sheriff, what are you yellin' about? Oh, hello there, may I help you folks?" she asked looking at the men standing on the steps. Frank Winthrop stepped up on the porch.

"Yes, Miss Daisy, I am Frank Winthrop. My son and I are looking for a hotel for my wife and young lady school teacher to rent. We thought you might have something."

"Well, Mr. Winthrop, on Saturday nights my hotel is filled with rowdy cowboys, no harm in them you understand, but they do get noisy. I don't think your wife would like it." He stepped back to the stairs and turned to Brad.

"No, Son, this wouldn't be the right place for your mother and our new school teacher."

Daisy heard a school teacher, she turned and replied, "Did you say a school teacher Mr. Winthrop?"

Mr. Winthrop turned back to her. "Yes, Miss Daisy, but it wouldn't be the place for either of these ladies. I also have my daughter-in-law and two granddaughters, so we would need a quiet place for them"

"Well, wait just a minute you see there is a house I own just beyond the school house. If you'd be interested, I could either rent it to you or sell it if you're interested in buying."

"Miss Daisy if the town is full of rowdy cowboys on the weekends I don't think we would want to move here even if there is a school house and it does need a school teacher. You see, Miss Daisy, we have two school teachers and want them to be comfortable in their living quarters as well as the town."

"Oh, yes, I understand Mr. Winthrop. Let me think on it, maybe I would consider selling you my hotel. We do need school teachers here, there are five or six farms on down in the holler who have enough children to more than fill the little school house."

"Why would you want to sell? It's filled on Saturdays, Miss Daisy?" Brad asked her. Waiting for an answer, Swift Eagle and Randy had stepped back down on the road.

"You see I also have three daughters living on the farms along the way and my grandchildren need an education. We gave up when the teacher moved to New York five years ago. Does it answer your question?"

Frank looked at his son and Randy, "What do you fellows think?"

"Dad, Mother wouldn't like living in the town if it was rowdy on any night you know how she is in Boston."

"Oh, my God you're from Boston! Come on in let's have some coffee and get acquainted. You see, I too, was born there and moved here with my late husband, God rest his soul."

They followed her into the large sitting room, it was comfortable with over stuffed couches and chairs. Apparently it had been a bawdy house at one time. She came back with a coffee pot and cups. She placed it on the table in the center of the room along with powdered milk and sugar. Swift Eagle had gotten used to things now, he helped himself to the coffee and sugar. Miss Daisy knew his buckskins told he was an Indian, yet was this man's grandson was a half breed. If they had money, which she now was sure they did have, she would close the rooming and boarding house. The cowboys could go to the house just outside of the town. She could quickly convert it into a boarding house just not as many rooms. Saturday nights, the cow hands wanted to let off steam and relax, no gun play or fights, they knew Sheriff Buck Henry would lock them up in a second in his one room jail.

Mr. Winthrop looked around and then said, "Brad, what do you say son, shall we take a look around?"

Brad stood up, Randy and Swift eagle joined them. They looked the rooms over. They were clean and had a dresser, bed, and chair each room. The kerosene lamp hung on a chain overhead and the only person to light it was Miss Daisy, because she felt it wouldn't get knocked over and cause a fire. There was a window in the six rooms up stairs and six down stairs. Large kitchens with a large wood stove, a pitcher pump, a wash basin on a bench, towels on a rack, cabinets for the dishes, pots, and pans, and a long table to work on.

The small room off from the kitchen had a large metal tub for taking a bath, where the water could be heated for the bath, poured into the tub and another pitcher pump in the room to cool the hot water in the tub.

The out house or privy was out back, available from either of the outside stairs or the downstairs hallway back door. There was always a catalog or corn shucks in the privy.

There was a small privy off to the side for the ladies. Miss Daisy pointed out the smoke house where she kept smoked hams and sausages hanging, her chicken yard furnished eggs and fried chicken especially on Sundays. Back from it was the dairy house she had glass quart jars full of canned beans, tomatoes, corn and peaches. There were always plenty of canned vegetables. She had help when the crops came in to help her can vegetables, butcher, smoke hams, and salt down slabs of pork bellies, it was in a cool place under giant live oak trees.

"This is very interesting, Miss Daisy. I can see how you are very well stocked."

She then suggested the return to the living room.

"Miss Daisy, we would like to rent four of your rooms tonight" Mr. Winthrop told her.

"Yes, Sir, I guess you would want the main floor?"

Bradley looked at the others, Swift Eagle just sat there, the others agreed, he would go along with their decision. After all he was used to sleeping on the ground.

Frank said, "Well, now it's settled." He then stood up and looked at Sheriff Buck Henry. "Sheriff, if you have the key to the school house would you be kind enough to show it to us?"

"Oh, yes, of course, fellers, come on lets go take a look at the old school house." Miss Daisy decided to come along with them. She now was definitely interested in these men and who cared if the grandson is a half breed, we need a school here and teachers. Wel,l she thought he seems like a well-adjusted man to her, this Swift Eagle. It's a good thing she never knew what happened to the men who raped his sister and killed his father. Oh well, they needed teachers so the children could have an education.

Sheriff Henry reached over the top of the door finding the key, then unlocked the front door. They went in the room was dusty and cobwebs. It would need some cleaning. There were windows all up and down each side to let in as much light as possible. The men stood there saying nothing, just looking the room over. There were thirty desks in front the teacher desk and chair, a black board across the wall behind the desk. Randy thought this is a far cry from the class rooms in Boston, but Mr. Winthrop offered me enough to compensate for the inconvenience this would bring Miss Lane and myself teaching. He thought maybe somehow they could divide the room into separate sections with half the desks on each side. If Mr. Winthrop decided on moving here, then he would suggest this to him. They soon were ready to leave. The school had an out door privy for the students, there was a pitcher pump and well at the front near the steps, and a large water troth. The men stood outside looking around, there were other buildings in the distance beyond Calhoun's bar.

Mr. Winthrop looked at the sheriff and asked, "Sheriff, what are the buildings on down the road from the Calhoun's?"

"Well, lets see, um first there's the General Mercantile shop, then we have a small grocery store, the goods come in once a month for both stores Miss Liberty is next, she has a dress and dry goods store, does alterations, has trousers, shoes, and helps serve as waitress at the hotel and Calhoun's on Saturdays and Sundays."

"Now where is your bank, Sheriff?"

The Sheriff looked over at Frank Bradley and said, "Sir, we don't have a bank. No one here has enough money to start a bank."

Brad looked at his dad, he wondered if they were both thinking the same thing.

"Um, Brad, what do you think? Could we organize and arrange to finance a bank here in Black Water?"

"You know it's many miles from out main holdings in Boston, Dad."

"Yes, it is and it takes two months by stage coach to travel to Boston from Fort McKinley.

"I have heard though, Dad, the train will soon be coming to Tennessee."

"Yes, I have read something in the Boston Herald about it some months ago."

The sheriff stopped and was looking amazed. He ran his hand across his unshaven face and mouth then said, "Uh, did I hear you correct, Mr. Winthrop, you and your son want to start a bank here in Black Water?"

"Yes, Sheriff, and our family member Swift Eagle has money of his own, with someone to guide and advise him to establish his own bank."

"My God, I can't believe this, a half breed Indian, with money he could start a bank."

Mr. Winthrop stood listening to this ignorant man. Brad stood looking down and kicking at the sand. Randy was quiet, how ignorant this man was. Of course, Swift Eagle didn't have any idea what was going on. He was used to the snide remarks of half breed, savage, injun, red skin. It didn't mean anything to him. He knew they meant him being an Indian. The fur trappers called him that. Randy wasn't amused at the ignorant remark.

At this time Swift Eagle was looking from Brad to his grandfather wondering what they were talking about, he wasn't sure what a bank was, could it be like Red Beard had with his box of money?

Finally, after a few moments in silence, Brad spoke up. "Dad, what do you say, let's go visit the other business places here?"

The sheriff overcame his disbelief this half breed had money in time to reply, "Oh, yes, Sir, let me introduce you folks to the others here in Black Water. We do have some fine people and the farmers on around the countryside who are God fearing church going people, too." He thought sure he would gain their attention then. They started walking toward the buildings.

The road was dusty. They could use some rain, Brad thought.

They came to the Mercantile Shop. The sheriff went up the steps, opened the screen door, it swung on squeaky hinges. As they entered the store it smelled of new clothing. Mr. Shufro had things arranged neatly. He was a little frame of a man who came from the back room smiling and greeted the men. "Good day gentlemen, please come in and look around. I am Myer Shufro. I will be glad to help you."

Mr. Winthrop went over and introduced himself, and then the others. The salesman and owner was polite and shook hands with the Indian before Swift Eagle made the first gesture.

Mr. Shufro said, "Can I get something for the young man, would you like to see some men's trousers, blue jeans, shoes, shirts, or even western boots and hats?"

"Well, you see I have been thinking of starting a bank here in Black Water, Mr. Shufro what would you think, would it be a good investment?."

Frank Winthrop knew this was an educated, intelligent man most likely moved here perhaps, from New York to open his business.

"Well, Sir, I would be interested in investing in such a venture should you decide. You see my wife and I moved here hoping the town would grow and we could also grow along with it."

"Very good idea, Mr. Shufro, I will certainly keep you in mind should we decide." They went to the door and on down the street. He stood at the door, watching as they walked to the next shop. It was on the opposite side of the street. The sign read, Black Water Grocery. They climbed the steps, the sheriff pushed the double screen doors they, too screeched open as they entered. It was clean and smelled of coffee, and neatly arranged with shelves on each side of the small store. A counter ran along one of the sides where the shelves behind it had coffee, sugar, flour, corn meal, and mostly dry food, the shelves on the opposite side were lined with cans of beans, condensed milk, corned beef, vegetable soup, and were sparsely stocked. A sign by the counter advertised salt pork, a hanging scale by the sign where it could be weighed. It was five cents a pound.

A lady came from the back, "Hello, Sheriff."

He went over to her and said, "Hello, Mrs. Brooks, I want you to meet some new comers to Black Water. He then introduced them.

She looked a moment at the Indian, and then said, "Welcome to Black Water friends, have you recently moved here?"

"No, Mrs Brooks, I am looking to see if my wife, Mrs. Winthrop, would be comfortable here. We are visiting here from Boston and she enjoys church each Sunday. I haven't met your pastor as yet though."

"Oh yes, Sir, well you see, my husband Mr. Brooks serves as our pastor for now, he is a carpenter by trade."

"Interesting. Is he around so we might meet Mr. Brooks?"

"No, Sir, he is building a barn for one of the families several miles down the way. He will be home for supper though if you would like to come back."

"Thank you, Mrs. Brooks, we are staying at Miss Daisy's hotel for the night. We may leave in the morning to Fort McKinley and then discuss if we are all interested in settling in Black Water."

The sheriff then spoke up and said, "Mrs. Brooks, these gentlemen have considered opening a bank here if they settle, also Mr. Randy Swain is a school teacher."

"Yes, it is interesting. Mr. Winthrop, how many persons you would need on the board if you decided."

"Well it depends on what they might wish to invest in a bank."

"If you decide to live in Black Water, please let me be one of your board members I can contribute to the finances needed."

"Thank you, Mrs. Brooks, you see my grandson, Swift Eagle would have the controlling interest should we decide."

Swift Eagle again wasn't surprised at her glancing at him. When they left the store he said, "Grandfather, me want white man clothes at store, and boots me have money?" He looked at Randy in his clothes. Randy could understand perfectly. He was glad Swift Eagle now understood.

"Yes, of course, Swift Eagle, come on let's go buy what clothes you want."

Brad grabbed his arm and hurried him off to the General Mercantile. The others had to run to catch up to them.

For the first time Randy laughed out loud, he had been very quiet and reserved, knowing what Swift Eagle was going through. Although he had been adopted as a small boy, he remembered some of the past he endured as an Indian. His English adoptive parents sent him to the very best schools and there was never any discrimination shown, his parents were Lord and Lady Swain. Randy never knew his other parents, he was found after their camp had been raided everyone killed. They hid him under fur pelts, some days later missionaries heard the infant crying, he was found and taken to the mission. He was adopted and went to England with his parent's, which is all he knew of his past. He could see how this man had a change to make in his life before him. He hoped he could help him.

Brad and Swift Eagle hurried to the mercantile store. Mr. Shufro came out front.

"Yes, Mr. Swift Eagle, can I help you?"

Brad waited for him to answer. Swift Eagle paused a moment, he was looking at the black boots on the counter in a box, he went over to them. They were too small then he looked at the clerk. He raised his foot and showed him.

"Ah, yes, Mr. Eagle, let me see what size boot you need."

Brad said, "Come over here, Swift Eagle, and sit down so he can try the boot on your foot."

The others were standing there by the door now watching. Mr. Shufro measured his foot and found a pair of which should fit, he brought a pair of socks.

"Here, Mr. Eagle, put your foot here." The man put his foot on a small table in front of the bench. He pulled the sock on and tried the boot, it fit perfectly. Mr. Shufro smiled as this young man was so happy with his first pair of boots.

"Whooe, Uncle Brad, whooe, boot, boot." They laughed at him. He was delighted with his boots and soon had the other one on walking around the counters. Mr. Winthrop came over, put his arm around Brad.

"Thank you, Son, this is a good day." He was thinking of his son, Frank. This was his son's child admiring his first pair of boots.

They finished with some blue denim jeans, denim shirts, under wear, a denim jacket, and western hat.

Randy was delighted at his friends happiness, he realized how fortunate he was.

Brad paid the man and they continued to the hotel. The evening found Swift Eagle dressed in western clothes and smiling broadly as they sat down to a large platter of fried chicken, a bowl of steamed rice, a bowl of gravy, platter of biscuits, blackberry jam, plenty of coffee, sugar and canned cream. After all Miss Daisy had good paying customers this evening. The hen house out back had chickens and eggs available.

Mr. Winthrop found the church services were held in the living room of Miss Daisy's hotel. They didn't have the church completed yet. Also, they never thought of a bank until now with this multi-millionaire here in town. After eating they went to the front room and sat to discuss what each one thought about moving to Black Water. Brad knew there would be hardships in moving here especially for his mother and he wasn't sure she would. He knew it was an opportunity to start a bank and get more activity here, He wondered what Randy was thinking about it. He looked his way and said, "Randy, what do you think about moving here to teach instead of the fort?"

"Well, Brad, the only thing is could we divide the classrooms. Miss Julie could teach either English or math but we would need to have separate classrooms. I will do what you and Mr. Winthrop want me to do."

They retired for the night. Swift Eagle slept in his new boots and jeans.

18

Early next morning found them enjoying a breakfast of ham, hot biscuits, scrambled eggs, and blackberry jam. After bidding Miss Daisy good bye, the early morning mist found them on the road to Fort McKinley. They would let the women know how things were in Black Water. Swift Eagle wondered what his mother and sisters would think of his new clothes and boots. He made sure though to keep his buckskins in a box by him. Quint was surprised to see his friend in the new clothes. He had his hair pulled tight at the back of his head. It was tied with a strip of buckskin. He thought it looked like Randy's hair cut.

Randy thought he looked very good in his first white man's clothes.

Mr. Winthrop was lost in his thoughts as they traveled along He knew he couldn't stay away from his business in Boston for any length of time. He would have to make some kind of arrangements to divide his time between both places if they should decide or else he would have to stay in Boston and let his son, Brad take care of things in Black Water. Then he thought the train would be coming to the south in the next couple or so years, he would wait and see. He and Brad would talk it over when they got to the fort, after they talked with the others. It would seem best for the school there, but his business would most assuredly have to be in Boston to take care of it financially.

They by passed the Dusty Road Trading Post on the return, it saved them at least another two hours on the road. They came into the gates of the fort around twelve noon. They were only too glad to get down turn the horses over to the soldiers and wash up. They noon meal had already been served. They were glad to have the left over beans, biscuits, and jam. Brad and Swift Eagle took their blankets and found a shady place by the wall of the fort, they lay there and rested. They would meet with Frank soon and discuss what their next move would be.

Brad wondered if Swift Eagle would be interested in taking his father's name. Frank Jr. it would be more simple to all concerned he thought, but he wasn't ashamed just thinking it easier to introduce him. He would ask him and see what he said.

Morning Star was amused seeing her son in the new clothes, the girls laughed and pointed to his new boots. He was delighted at the attention his boots got. One thing sure this young man wasn't ashamed of his new duds, he was delighted.

The men were invited to eat meals with the soldiers, the ladies were invited to the officer's mess hall.

The next day Frank ask the others to meet in the large room so they could discuss with everyone present the pros and cons of moving to Black Water and then leave it to the others to ask questions or discuss the opportunities there or disabilities in relocating there. This would be the move Morning Star and her children would make. They would be comfortable at the hotel. They would have to either get used to wearing clothing in place of the buckskins or whatever they chose to do. It would be easier to wash the cloth things than the buckskin clothing. This had to be discussed, too.

They met in the morning at the new room. Mr.Winthrop stood in the front of the room beside the desk the others sat on the benches.

He began, "I want you to understand, if you decide to move to Black Water it will be much different than living in your teepee in Lone Wolf's camp. If you do attend this school, you will have to live here at the fort because of the distance you couldn't travel each day, is that understood?" He stood silently waiting for what he said to sink in.

Morning Star and the girls knew it was meant for them in particular. It would mean complete strangers, they would be with and being Indian would be observed as different to the people there until they knew them and became used to their difference. The same would go for them to adjust to their new surrounding, no one they knew other than the teachers and Brad, if he decided to stay.

Morning Star knew she would have to sacrifice, yet knew if her son and daughters were to join the so called civilized world they had to learn to read, write, and speak with the white man's words. She looked at her daughters and her son. She then stood looking at Mr. Winthrop and said, "I will move to Black Water, Mr. Winthrop, father of my husband Frank."

The girls sat staring at her knowing they would move to a new place, no friends, and no teepees.

Brad then stood up and said, "Father, I would like to say something, if you don't mind."

"Of course, Son, you have the floor."

"I want to tell you, Morning Star, widow of my brother, I will stay in Black Water with you and the children until they have completed their education. After we will see what happens next, is it understood?"

Morning Star stood up then and replied, "Yes, Brother of my husband, I am glad you stay with us there," she sat down.

Brad looked over and said, "Well, I guess that settles it. Mother, we will all go and see the town of Black Water. We placed orders so when the stage coach comes I think it will bring some more books, pencils, writing tablets, and things we ordered. You and Father will then return to Boston. I will send another order for paper, pencils, chalk, erasers, history, English, and geography books. The next wagon or stage coach can deliver the things to Black Water."

"Then I will talk with Colonel Wesley and engage two of the horse and buggies to take us there. We will go to the hotel first, let you get settled, and meet Miss Daisy."

Frank stood then and said, "If there is nothing else to discuss, I will go see the colonel"

Brad said, "Father, I will come with you."

They left and the women were left to discuss their plans. Actually the girls were really excited and started asking Swift Eagle about the place, where he got the boots, his clothes, etc.

After Mr. Winthrop made arrangements for the two buggies they returned. It was time for Brad to broach the subject to Swift Eagle about being called Frank, Jr. Brad went over beside him and said, "Swift Eagle, have you ever thought your name could be Frank, Junior?"

"You say my name Frank like father's name?"

"Yes, what do you think about it?"

He was silent and looked at his mother then back at Brad. "It good name I like Frank, Junior, name."

The girls were thinking of new names now like Star for their mother and Sylvia for his sister and then Whitney. Yes, they decided to do the same thing. So now we had a Sylvia, Star, Frank, Jr., and Whitney.

They were excited gathering the things they would take with them. Of course Brad's mother, Mary Elizabeth, had her small suitcase and was ready. Colonel Wesley was relieved to know his star boarder and roomers would be leaving, for more reasons than one. The soldiers had an eye for the white girl and she was aware of the men. It would have been inconvenient to have them here at least two years. He was only too glad to furnish the horse and buggies and see them leave. The fort did have a covered wagon, but it had no springs every hole or stone it hit would be felt. Where the buggy had springs and might be crowded, but much more comfortable.

The journey would be tiresome for the ladies. They decided to start the following morning early. Mary Elizabeth would ride beside her husband who would hold the reins, Randy could sit on the floor of the buggy, and Julie the other side, with a blanket to sit on. Brad would hold the reins Star would ride by him, Whitney, and Sylvia on folded blankets, on the floor board. This way horses would be under the control of someone who knew how to handle them. So in the morning they would begin the trip to Black Water. The girls were excited, Star knew it was the only decision she could make, if her children were to have an opportunity in life.

The men had their weapons, Brad had his gun and Frank Jr. of course, could handle any situation, should one arise with either a four legged animal or one with two legs. It had been done before. They were perfectly safe for the trip.

They knew when Mary Elizabeth and Frank Winthrop were to leave Black Water it would be on the stage coach with an armed man riding shotgun for their safety.

The girls were thoroughly enjoying their ride through the woods road. Mary Elizabeth was enjoying the wild birds and small animals like rabbits, squirrels, every now and then a deer would jump across the path in front of them. The morning was cool and the scent of the wild flowers was nice on the morning air.

Julie was not bothered by sitting on the floor with Randy; teachers had endured much more incontinence than this. Really the ride wasn't bad at all. She also, was getting used to the ways of the country, if you could call it that. They arrived at Quint's blacksmith shop late afternoon. Quint was working in his shop. He stopped and came out to greet them. Brad introduced them. He helped take the horses to the corral. The group was grateful for fresh water and glad to walk and stretch their legs.

Quint was amazed seeing his friend Swift Eagle in white man's clothes. The group walked on to Miss Daisy's hotel. Brad went up to the door and knocked.

Miss Daisy came to the door. "Come in come in, welcome to Black Water. I am, Miss Daisy come and let's get you folks settled in."

They joined Miss Daisy in the living room. Julie quickly found a soft chair, Mary and Star also found a place to sit and relax. Miss Daisy stood there a moment then said, "Would you folks like some tea or coffee may be fresh water?"

Mary Elizabeth quickly answered, "Yes, Dear, I would love a cup of tea, thank you." The men also found a place on the couch to sit. The girls were looking around at the pictures on the walls in the living room. It wasn't unusual for Julie but for Star, Sylvia and Whitney it was strange to them. Most of them were photos of people. Of course, they had never been inside of a house like this before. Star was interested also. The Trading Post and Fort McKinley were the only places she had been in other than the teepee.

After enjoying the tea, each was shown to their room. Whitney and Sylvia wanted to share their room. Julie was glad to lie down and take a nap. Mary and Frank napped. Brad, Randy, and Frank, Jr. had rooms by each other. Frank Jr. wanted to talk with his Uncle Brad. He was in his uncle's room sitting by the bed. Brad slept while he kept on talking. Every so often the uncle would grunt uh huh, his nephew never slowed down, he was wound up.

Around dark, a bell awakened them, "Come to dinner, come to dinner." Miss Daisy called out.

Brad got up washed his face and joined the others in the dining room.

They were all in the dining room. Miss Daisy had a table set with fried chicken, biscuits, mashed potatoes, and gravy,

A large bowl of fresh picked snap green beans, seasoned with hog jowl, and hoe cake of corn bread, hot coffee, cream, and sugar.

They sat at the long table. Mr. Frank Winthrop was at the end of the long table. They looked his way. He bowed his head and said a brief blessing, thanking the Almighty for their safe trip and this lovely dinner prepared by Miss Daisy. Whitney glanced over at Sylvia. Every one enjoyed the food none was left over. Finally, they retired to the living room. The girls helped Miss Daisy wash dishes and put them away. They giggled and went to the outhouse before retiring, for the night. Morning Star looked over at them and then retired herself for the night.

The men sat in the living room after dinner talking.

Sheriff Henry joined them evening. He was astonished at the ladies. They were different from what he expected. He let them know he would meet the men in the morning to open the school house and there were people hearing of them going to open the school. They wanted to help clean the room and windows, one man came with paint to do the inside and out-side walls, the others to wash the floors and clean windows. The ladies just took a look inside then went to see Mr Shufro's mercantile store.

Then, of course, they met Mrs. Brooks. She told them the little store beside her was a seamstress and dressmaking shop. Miss Leila Clark, owned it she stocked bolts of cloth gingham and many other lovely patterns. Julie wanted her to make two new dresses for her. Now it was the Indians girls' turn. Star, Sylvia, and Whitney were all fitted for dresses. They bought shoes at the mercantile. They excitedly returned to the hotel with their goodies. The girls had found a couple of dresses and the black patent shoes with button straps. They never had a pair of shoes in their lives or any thing other than buckskin dress. Star, in the privacy of her room quietly tried on the dress, she wanted, her shoes, and cotton stockings, they were also sold cotton under wear, (bloomers) Sylvia looked at Whitney and laughed. And under skirts, the lady told her how to wear them. Star placed the bloomers in a shoe box by the foot of the bed after pulling on the stockings, she slowly put her feet into the black patent leather shoes. They were beautiful. The ladies had boots with buttons, they liked the shiny black shoes the best. She put her dress on and it felt so soft against her skin. It was blue, plaid, gingham and had buttons down the front to match the blue. She wondered how Tall Man Frank, would have liked it on her. She admired the dress in the mirror in the room.

The next morning the sheriff was with the others at the school yard, everyone was doing something.

The men were busy cleaning the school house, even Mr. Winthrop helped. He was raking the grounds, cleaning the cob webs from inside the two privies, one for the boys and the other the girls. He was cutting brush from around the buildings. The men stopped at lunch time to enjoy some biscuits and fried salt pork. After taking a brief rest, they went back to work. The bell tower was next, Quint had a ladder which would reach. It was taken down and new braces to hold it were put in place, then a new rope to pull it with. It rang loud and clear, if the farmer's children wished to attend, they could hear it for miles. After the floor dried, Randy took his box of books, spelling tablets, paper, pencils, chalk, and placed them on the desk at the front of the room. It was a start. The men then moved the student desks to opposite sides. The carpenter, Mr. Brooks, had some unplaned boards donated to divide the room into separate classrooms. Then Miss Daisy donated one of her dining room tables and chairs for the other room. Julie would have that room to start with. Mr. Winthrop had already ordered a new desk and chair for the separate class room. The teachers would decide which classes they would start with. Randy knew the Indians had no education at all in writing or numbers. They discussed taking them by themselves to begin with and if other children came they would find out how much schooling each one had and place them in which class they should be in.

People came to the hotel the next day with the children. They were families from the farms in the area. They introduced themselves, glad to have the school open again.

They told Mr. Winthrop they would welcome a doctor from Boston when he and his wife returned, any young person wishing to start a practice would be welcome here in Black Water. Brad knew they should build a bank and he talked with, Mr. Brooks, the minister, and carpenter in the town. Where would they get the material to build it? He found another small rural town had a saw mill and they could order what kind of boards and two by fours or what size timbers they wished to build the bank. They were busy doing these things as time went by.

Mrs. Mary Winthrop busied her time visiting with Miss Leila Clark, the seamstress, and Mrs. Brooks, of course, spending time on the lovely front porch enjoying the afternoons. In the meantime, Star was learning how to run the kitchen from

Miss Daisy, how she did the canning, had help slaughtering the stock for the hams, those she hired to help her with the canning, preserving, hams, bacon, making sausages, and keeping the fire in the smoke house just at the proper temperature.

Whew, Star thought, *there was so much to learn about owning and managing a hotel and boarding house.*

The school now had twenty students including the four Indians. Whitney had learned to write her name as did Star Winthrop, so did Sylvia, Frank Jr. They had learned the ABC letters reading the words, cat, dog, man, boy, girl. Randy ask Frank, Jr. to stand up and read the first line in one of their books. He looked around and slowly stood up, opened the book and read, "The dog ran down the road."

Star was so proud of her son, he was the first one to read in school. When the stage rolled in Mr. and Mrs. Frank Winthrop had seen the bank completed with a sign on the front. Winthrop Bank of Black Water. They had a wooden sidewalk in front of the bank. Now the other store owners were having sidewalks in front of their stores. Another hotel was built at the far end of town. The Winthrop's had purchased Miss Daisy's hotel. Calhoun had another hotel built outside of town to be sure the cowhands had a place to stay on Saturday nights after spending their money in his saloon. He hired a bartender who could play two tunes on his old piano. The wagon from the fort came once a month. It brought things the people in the town ordered as well as a desk, chair, cabinets, and supplies when it came. The farmers now raised most of the potatoes and stored them in the barns.

Brad's mother and dad had been here almost a year. They would be leaving on the next Wells Fargo stage coach this next week. He hated to see them go but knew his dad had to get back to their business. They would keep in touch by the

Pony Express. Things were beginning to look as if the railroad would be coming this way soon. Which would certainly cut down travel time, inconveniences for the passengers, no outside privies, and could have meals on the train not having to stop at the relay stations to eat.

Brad decided to stay on in Black Water. When the rails did come through to the closest town, then he could go visit them in Boston. Now he was busy with the bank and Frank Jr. was more like Randy in his manner and actions. His mother, Star, had learned to sew and was helping the seamstress, Miss Leila in her little shop. The girls had learned to read and write and were working in Calhoun's, Whitney as a waitress, serving meals and Sylvia at the hotel also a waitress. Sylvia's intended husband, Strong Bow had somehow made it to Black Water. He was working for Quint in the black smith shop. He had not as yet adopted the white man's clothes and boots as had his friend, (Swift Eagle) now Frank Jr.

After the Winthrop's returned to Boston, he talked to his doctor and told him the need for a doctor in Black Water. The ole doc.having delivered most of the children around the area, decided he would go to Black Water. He had a young intern he talked to and who decided also he wanted to go with Doctor Jones. .He was not married and looking for some place to put up his shingle, Doctor James Young M.D to begin his practice. The way Mr. Winthrop described the rural town of Black Water, they didn't have a doctor now and didn't have a bank until they organized the Winthrop Bank of Black Water. Yes, it seemed an opportunity for a young doctor just starting his practice. The two doctors packed their medical equipment and medicines they planned to catch the next stage coach heading to Fort McKinley and Black Water.

The ladies at the church Mary Elizabeth attended wanted her to address the ladies social group and tell them all about Black Water and those who lived there. She was delighted to be the center of attention. They met at her residence. She graciously had her maid and butler serve refreshments for the ladies. The meeting was a success and made the local newspaper society column. They also were planting flowers in the park and beautifying their city. Mary Elizabeth was glad to be home. Frank Winthrop joined his friends and associates at the Business Men's Club, after seeing to his finances and books. He was satisfied they were in order and the ship yard was in good shape, his financial adviser went over things with him.

He was invited to speak on his year at Black Water and what he had done there. Frank told them of the school and organizing the Winthrop Bank of Black Water. His fellow members were visibly impressed. He told them his grandson, Frank Jr. invested a large sum and his son, Brad and the town's people also invested in the bank. The town needed a hospital, a doctor, a dentist, and barber shop. It was a growing community and when the rails came through it would grow rapidly. There were many opportunities in the town, his son planned to live there. The bank was able to make loans for building houses and the interest was what the investors wanted. They, of course, had questions about his son, Frank's, half breed children and widow. Frank was only too eager to tell all about them. He was proud of Frank's children and his daughter in law, Star Winthrop.

20

Mr. Brooks had been conducting services at the hotel on Sundays, an attractive young lady had been attending the Sunday services in Winthrop's living room, always alone. Brad paid particular attention to her.

She was very quiet and a petite, beautiful, young lady who wasn't shy. The group met after Mr. Brooks' services and everyone enjoyed a dinner usually of fried chicken, biscuits, and gravy. The meal was by donation and if you didn't have any money, it was free. Brad and Frank Jr. picked up the tab.

Her name was Lynett Webster. Brad had wanted to marry again, but hadn't found anyone until now he thought might be compatible. He wanted to invite her to go for a buggy ride with him, but wasn't sure if she would think him bold.

Star could see her brother-in-law was interested in this lady. She could see Lynette cast glances at Brad when he wasn't aware of it. She decided to let Brad know the lady was interested in him. He was delighted to know it. Which gave him the courage he needed. After dinner they were sitting on the porch, Brad thought it's now or never. He looked over at her and said, "Miss Webster, I wonder if you would like to go for a ride through the countryside with me this afternoon." There he had said it, now waiting for a reply.

She turned smiling at him and replied, "Why yes, thank you, Mr. Winthrop. I would enjoy a ride through the country with you."

Star was watching from the window in the living room, she smiled thinking of his brother Frank was shy like Brad, but she caught his eye and married him.

Brad then told Lynette, "I will go bring my rig, Miss Webster. I will only be a few minutes."

"I will be waiting right here, Mr. Winthrop," She smiled at him.

He soon returned with his new buggy with isinglass curtains which could roll down in case of rain. And his beautiful white mare, he bought from one of the cowboys. He boarded it with Quint and left his buggy there, too. Quint who was glad to have the extra income.

Star came out on the porch, "It's a beautiful afternoon isn't it, Mrs. Winthrop?"

"Yes, Miss Webster, it is. Oh, here comes Brad with his buggy. How nice, and you're going for a ride this afternoon."

Brad pulled up to the porch, got down, and threw the reins over the hitching rail. He went up the steps and said, "Oh, hello, Star, isn't this a lovely afternoon?"

She smiled at him from the porch swing.

Brad looked over at Lynette, "Are you ready, Miss Webster?"

She stood up, taking his arm as they went down the steps to his new buggy and white mare. They were quite handsome.

She admired them, "Mr. Winthrop, your rig is quite nice."

"Thank you, Miss Webster. I really like it."

He helped Lynette up into the buggy, went to the other side, and climbed in beside her.

"Good afternoon, Star, we will see you later."

Star waved to them as he drove on up the road Miss Webster by his side. She had on a lovely perfume. It smelled, he thought of the sent soft cinnamon and cedar, a lovely clean fresh scent. The afternoon ride was perfect she even moved closer to this handsome man thankful he had invited her on this ride with him today.

Now that Sylvia could read and write, wearing the white people's shoes and clothes, Strong Bow had feelings of inferiority. He shied away from her. She was different, he loved her, and couldn't understand. Quint told him he could learn to read and write also if he would talk to Randy, after all Randy was an Indian, too. It gave Strong Bow some encouragement, but he had to think about it now.

21

Several months after the Winthrop's returned to Boston the stage coach from Boston came, bringing the two doctors. The driver pulled in at the Winthrop House. Brad met the coach and greeted the two doctors. He took their luggage to the porch. After formally introducing them to his sister-in-law, he brought their luggage and showed them to their rooms. The Winthrop House as it was now known had very special guests. To be sure when Doctor James Young came in the next morning, at breakfast, Whitney's heart skipped a beat. She looked down quickly as if she hadn't noticed him. To be sure he had seen both the young ladies.

She hadn't given the braves or men she had seen even a second glance. Star noticed her daughter and really felt quite satisfied to know her white daughter showed an interest in this man. Her Indian daughter still loved her brave. She just wanted him to get more education, too.

The next morning Brad came in with Doctor Jones and Doctor Young. They stopped at the dining room, "Good morning, everyone. I want to introduce Doctor Jones and Doctor Young." Everyone looked up, Brad continued, "Gentlemen you have met my sister-in-law, Mrs. Star Winthrop, who manages our home and hotel to special guest as yourselves."

"Good morning, Mrs. Winthrop."

"Come and have breakfast with us, my daughters Whitney and Sylvia."

The girls looked up and smiled.

"I am Doctor James Young. I am glad to meet you both." He sat down where Star had set a cup of coffee for each of them.

"Yes, and I am Doctor Forest Jones, almost retired, but Mr. Frank Winthrop more or less convinced me Black Water could use an old man doctor and this young feller wanted to come along with me."

"We are so glad to have you both here with us," Star replied.

Brad stood amazed at what his sister-in-law said. She was certainly learning to speak well.

As they sat at breakfast, Doctor Young glanced at Whitney. He then asked, "Miss Whitney, where do you work?"

She looked over her cup of coffee, and replied, "Doctor Young, I am a waitress at Calhoun's restaurant and bar down the road."

"I was asking because I will need a nursing assistant when I open my office and practice. I wondered if you would be interested in being trained as a nursing assistant, both myself and Doctor Jones would be glad to train you."

"Oh, Doctor Young, I would also like to train for a nurse," Sylvia spoke up.

"Why yes, Doctor Young, I certainly would be interested, when could we start?"

He laughed, "Well, Miss Whitney, and Miss Sylvia, give me time to catch my breath and find a proper place for an office. Once we're set up I know we can use more nurses and need more space to build a hospital. There are never enough good nurses."

Sylvia said, "Oh, yes, of course, Doctor Young, I was over eager."

Star joined the conversation now, "Excuse me, Doctor. I do have a front room you might be interested in making into an office for now. It could be divided or our living room could be used as a waiting room."

Doctor Jones now joined in, "What a great idea, Mrs. Winthrop. After breakfast, would you show us the room please?"

Sylvia sat quiet, saying nothing, hoping she, too could train with Whitney and become a nurse. After everyone finished breakfast, the girls helped wash dishes and put things away. Star showed the doctors the room. There was an adjoining room which would be handy if they had an emergency, like surgery. They would have much work to get the rooms in order and painted white throughout, including the ceiling and board floor.

They knew it was large enough to divide and make both examining room and waiting room. There was an adjoining room which could be used as sort of hospital room, if needed.

Doctor Jones left an order in Boston for the next stage coach or wagon whichever came first to deliver. It would have the needed supplies: chloroform, iodine, swabs, and mercury, soap, for sanitizing their hands, cotton, gauze bandages, and adhesive tape. The doctors the needed drugs with them: laudanum, Sloas liniment, tables, cabinets, and they could be assembled once they arrived.

Brad knew they should hold a meeting at the school house to introduce the doctors to the community. They would do it the next day. Of course, the store owners had seen the stage coach when the men came in. The news had spread already throughout the rural farms. They knew when they heard the bell sounding, a meeting was called. Frank Jr. went to Quint's and borrowed one of his horses. He rode to the farms and let them know there would be a meeting at the school tonight and meet the new doctors in town.

22

The bell ringing out over the countryside at seven in the evening gave the people in the outlying area time to get to the meeting at the school house.

By eight o'clock the school room was filled with the citizens of Black Water and people within hearing distance of the ringing bell. Brad was at the front desk. The doctors sat on each side. After everyone was seated or standing. Brad raised his hand. When they quieted down he began, "Good evening, everyone. I called this meeting to introduce you to the new residents. I know you will be glad to welcome Doctors Forest Jones, he stood up and James Young to Black Water. I know they will be glad to answer any questions you have and tell you where they will have their office set up. Please welcome Doctor Forest Jones." He stood up as Brad paused a moment for applause then continued, "And welcome Doctor James Young." He stood up, the audience applauded, and quieted as Doctor Jones held up his hand.

"Good evening, thank you for your welcome, we are glad to be here in Black Water. You may not know this, but when Mr. Frank Winthrop returned to Boston he advised me a medical doctor was needed here. I was ready to retire, but thought I may be of some help to you folks. My fellow associate, Doctor Young, asked if he might accompany me. Please meet, Doctor Young."

He stood as they applauded both men.

"Thank you. Thank you, fellow citizens. I am happy to join you I hope we may be of help. I understand Mrs. Brooks has done an excellent job of serving as midwife to deliver your babies. I hope we can be of assistance, also and have a little medication to help relieve some pain. Are there any questions you would like to ask?"

"Yes, Sir, where will you have an office?"

Doctor Young replied, "We will have offices in the Winthrop House on the first floor."

"When will your office open for business, Doctor?" one of the ladies stood and asked, it was obvious she was with child.

"We will be ready to deliver your baby when you're ready."

Everyone laughed.

"Will you come to my home or will it be here in the office?"

"We have made arrangements for a delivery room but, unless this is your first child I should say at your home."

"Thank you, Doctor Young." She sat down.

"Are there any other questions?"

"Yes, Sir. I hope you will pull teeth, too, Doctor Young."

"Well, if there isn't a dentist I would say yes."

"Do we have to get drunk to have them pulled?"

Everyone laughed again.

"No, I don't think that's necessary, we have chloroform and laudanum to ease the pain."

"Whew, Doc, that's a relief to know," he sat down.

Doctor Jones stood up and said, "Fellow citizens, if there are no more questions, I suggest we enjoy some of Mrs. Winthrop and her daughter's cake and coffee they made especially for this meeting."

Star spoke up saying, "Line up and I will serve each of you."

Star knew there would be a crowd she made at least a dozen cakes and gallons of coffee. They all came to the front where they formed a line and were soon enjoying the treat. Star sliced cake, placed it on plates, and the girls poured the coffee. Everyone was talking, kids running around, peeking at the doctors, and wondering about them. Some of the kids had been told the doctor brought the babies in their satchel. The meeting was a success. The folks drove their teams and families on home. Doctors Young and Jones retired to their respective rooms at the Winthrop House. It was good meeting, the fine folks of Black Water gave them a warm welcome, and they felt it.

Next day the men were busy arranging things in the two rooms a desk and chair in the one room another couple of chairs where the patients could wait. They wished to have the walls painted and Mr. Brooks agreed to do the job they wanted all white interior paint in the rooms. Things progressed very well for now. Miss Webster was given a job as teller in the bank, she had gone to school at the University of Wisconsin and knew financial matters and advanced math. Brad ask Randy to serve sort of as accountant to see over the books. Brad conferred with Frank Jr. who agreed to increase Randy's salary. During this time Randy was teaching the girls and Frank Jr. the history of the United States, of course they knew how the Indians had been and were being treated by the white government, but they also learned how the Negro had been and was still being treated. Along the way they learned good manners and how to ignore the remarks ignorant people (like Colonel Wesley) made. Of course, Frank Jr. had never until now known any different. He had taken it for granted and it didn't mean anything to him. .Now under Randy's teaching they were understanding the white people were not being nice to them but insulting. The education would make all the difference in their lives.

23

Sheriff Buck Henry had noticed some strange men, hanging around Calhoun's restaurant and bar. They had wandered in during the night. He went over to the bar to talk with Calhoun. The same men were at the bar when he came in. They stopped talking and looked over at the sheriff.

"Hey Sheriff, how's everything?" Calhoun greeted him, he walked over to the bar where these strangers were.

"Hey, Calhoun, I come to find out who our strangers are."

The strangers looked around at him. The sheriff could see they were carrying guns. The big, burly, unshaven man looked around at Sheriff Buck Henry and said, "You talkin' bout us, Sheriff?"

"Yes, Sir, where are you from?"

"We come from the coal mines, it caved in, and we were out of work so headed this way."

"Where're your horses or did you walk all that way?" He could see the men were getting edgy. Calahoun pulled his double barrel 12 gauge closer to the edge of the shelf, under the bar. He stood waiting to see what next.

"No we sold them to the black smith at the edge of town."

"Well, Fellas, I suggest you buy them back and keep on ridin.' There's nothing in Black Water for you."

"We don't want any trouble, Sheriff, just to have a drink and find some work."

"Like I said, there's nothin' here for you. We are just a small town no mines or ranches, get your drink and head on out."

Sheriff Henry put his hand on the gun at his hip and stood waiting. These fellows knew this man meant what he said. They paid Calhoun and headed back to Quints to get the horses they claim to have sold. Sheriff Henry followed.

Brad was at the bank and had seen the strangers go by. He stopped the sheriff, "I don't like the looks of these men, Sheriff, I am going to go see Frank Jr. He is at Quint's now."

They both followed the strangers to Quints, they were saddling up the mounts which were worn out already. Frank Jr. was at the anvil hammering on a horse shoe, but keeping his attention on the strangers all the while. They walked their mounts to the edge of town.

Quint came to Sheriff Henry saying, "Sheriff, those mounts were stolen from the Smoky Range Ranch. I saw the brand on them."

Frank Jr. quickly changed to his moccasins and buckskins, he always kept his special made knife in the sheath at his waist whether in civilian or buckskin clothes. Quint had the horse bridled handing Frank Jr. the reins he mounted Quint's horse bare back riding toward the Smoky Range Ranch. He wanted to find out exactly what was going on and if anyone was hurt there.

Sheriff Henry went to the school house and rang the bell to summon the farmers. The men came quickly on horse back to the school house. Sheriff Henry stood on the steps telling them about the six men and the stolen horses they were riding.

Amos stood up and said, "They came by my place and tried to corral one of mine. I came out with my shotgun and they started running."

"You're lucky. Amos. They could have killed you."

"Not with my loaded ole double barrel. The last I saw they had gone into the woods road, but those horses can't go far. I am thinkin' them guys will double back here."

"All right men now you know what to be lookin' for. We will go together and see if we can find them."

In the meantime Frank jr. arrived to find one of the cow-hands dead on the ground. The others had been wounded and the women were hiding in the storm cellar. He called to them. They came out crying and telling him what happened. These men had robbed the bank and killed the guard in the town of Red Hill. Frank Jr. told the women to get food and water, stay in the cellar. He until help come. Then he helped the wounded men to the cellar.

He headed back to Black Water. His mother told him the men had formed a posse and headed to find these men. Frank, Jr. changed horses and road out to join them. He could hear the guns in the distance, so circled around through the woods. This was home to Swift Eagle. When he got closer he saw they had taken a little girl hostage with a gun to her head. Sheriff Henry and the posse tried to reason with them to let the girl go.

Swift Eagle crept slowly along. He could see the girl, raised his bow, and waited. When the man took the gun away from her head, Swift Eagle sent the arrow straight into the man's neck. He dropped the girl and fell to the ground screaming, pulling at the arrow. Swift Eagle was right there, picked the girl up, and rode with her in his arms to the posse. Her father was screaming and crying until he saw his daughter safe with Swift Eagle.

Swift Eagle (Frank Jr.) quickly turned and raced to see if he could stop the other killers as they scattered, running wildly into the woods. This was old stuff to him. He might wear white man's clothes and boots now, but he knew how to deal with this kind of renegade. He saw another one sneaking along the underbrush, Swift Eagle slid down from the horse, crouching, lifted the bow, inserted the arrow, and sent it swiftly into the man's shoulder.

The man stood up screaming, pulling at the arrow sticking out of his shoulder. The others continued running wildly through the brush. As they did Swift Eagle raised his head and "Aieee, Aiee." They wondered what the hell the sound was. Achill went through them.

Brad knew what it was. He just stood silent watching as they tried to catch the rest of the killers. They had heard stories of an Indian called Death Wind, so many years ago. Legend was when he caught the one who killed his father and raped his sister, he killed them violently. He dragged this one out to the posse. Where they strapped him onto the mule they brought along. The others were now surrounded and the farmers tied them to their horses and rode double back to town. The posse wondered what the sound was they heard but kept silent about it.

For sure this group would hang. Black Water had a hanging tree by the blacksmith shop. Of course, they would have the folks who survived the attack at Smoky Range Ranch to be witness.

The little jail now was full. Brad now knew the town would need a larger one. They would use the school house for the trial. Brad heard about the arrows in the renegade and knew exactly what that sound was. He had heard it before.

The two with arrow wounds were patched up by Doctor Young who was amazed at the accuracy in which the arrows missed the bone. He performed surgery to get the arrow heads out.

"Who do these arrow heads belong to, Sheriff?"

"Well Doc, they belong to Swift Eagle, Mr. Winthrop's grandson. "

"My God! It's unbelievable. Would you give them to him please?" He handed them to Sheriff Henry who stood by with shot guns until the men were safely in the jail.

There were some angry people who didn't want to have a trial. They didn't have a judge or attorney in Black Water. Sheriff Henry wasn't concerned.

Brad didn't get into it except for riding with the posse, shivering when he heard his nephews sound echoing through the forest. This was one Indian nobody wanted on their trail.

After meeting with the citizens, it was decided to proceed with the trial. They would build a scaffold to hang all six of them at the same time. There was only one hangin tree back of Quint's blacksmith shop.

Sheriff Henry had Brad come to the office to call a town meeting the next evening to decide on a judge. Then he asked those witness to sign a paper and asked the citizens to appoint a judge. They murmured in low voices until Mr. Brooks stood saying, "We decided that Mr. Shufro is the only one in town not prejudiced."

They wanted him as the judge. He pleaded with them to find someone else, but they stood firm. The trial was set for the next week when the two injured men would be recovered from their wounds. The little school house was filled with the citizens and rural folks waiting to see the out come of the murders and kidnapping of the little girl. The witness and the others side were in the school house. One of the farmers stood with his shotgun by the door.

Swift Eagle stood by, David Brooks who would be one juror, since he was preacher, carpenter, and business owner. The others were business people and farmers. Brad wanted someone who wasn't in the posse to serve as judge. The townspeople agreed with Brad, Myers Shufro would be judge.

Mr. Shufro didn't want to be judge. The town insisted. He was a religious, quiet, and reserved man. They thought would be perfect to judge of witnesses' testimony of the incidents. Of course, they had a jury to listen to the evidence and determine the verdict and punishment for the men.

The day of the trial the town was full of people who came from all around Black Water. Calhoun's was busy frying chicken and baking biscuits. Star did the same having to hire some help from the folks who helped smoke the hams and do the canning to be sure there was enough to feed everyone in town. The trial started early in the morning.

They heard from the widow of Bill South, he was gunned down as the six rode into their yard. The other cowhands didn't have their guns on and took shelter in the barn as the six men fired at them and stole their horses. The ranch hands were taken by surprise. They were branding cattle when the six rode in. Mr. South went to greet whomever they were and was gunned down.

The intruders kept firing. The wounded crawled to the barn. The ladies in the house ran for the storm cellar and hid there. At first hearing them coming, they thought it was friends. Then the man whose daughter was abducted testified. The jurors knew a horse thief was already due to hang. This was the law of the west.

They then turned to Judge Shufro the foreman of the jury said, "Judge, we members of this jury find these men guilty and sentence them to death by hanging."

Everyone was looking at Myer Shufro, who sat silent, his head looking down a few moments, raised up then said, "Jurors is this your final verdict after hearing the witness and their testimony?"

The courtroom was silent waiting for the foreman, Bart Lane to answer. He had talked with the jurors after the witness had testified. They all agreed to hanging for the murder of Rancher South, as well as stealing the horses, and kidnapping the child.

Swift Eagle though he could have saved them a lot of time, if they had turned them loose. He didn't agree, but this was the white man's way. He stood waiting to see what Myer Shufro had to say.

Judge Myers looked over his glasses at the crowd there in the school room.

"Ladies and gentlemen I am a quiet, calm man, and abhor violence. Under the circumstances and the testimony of the witness I can see no other verdict except guilty for these men. I would then instruct Sheriff Buck Henry and his deputies, to do as the law declares, to hang these men." He bowed his head, turned and looked at the six men saying, "You have been found guilty by this court and will hang by the neck until dead. May God have mercy on your souls?" Judge Shufro stepped away from the desk and headed for the door as the crowd cheered and clapped. He left the room his head bowed as he slowly walked down the road to his shop, went in, and shut the door to everyone. He would spend the rest of the day in prayer asking forgiveness for his part in this trial.

Sheriff Buck Henry and the deputies as well as, David Brooks and Brad Winthrop were appointed to be present at the hanging. Brad wasn't keen about this, but had read about such things in the western novels before coming to the west. These were murderers, bank robbers, and horse thieves, jeopardizing the little girl's life as a hostage.

The sheriff and deputies dragged them to the wagon, Quint drove them on to the scaffolds. Quint stood guard, Swift Eagle watched in case they needed a hand as they were lifted and the noose placed around their neck while their hands and feet were tied. The sheriff pulled the rope to the trap door. Brad turned away, his nephew Swift Eagle, didn't bat an eye knowing it was less painful than what he would have given them. They stayed around for a while after doing their duty. These renegades were no longer a menace to any one in this area.

This was unpleasant to Brad, yet he knew this was the unwritten law. Swift Eagle could see his uncle Brad was sick at the sight of the men hanging. What would he think if he had seen his brother having been knifed and left to die slowly? Would he not want justice for his brother? He thought it certainly wasn't the way it was done in Boston his Uncle Brad would get used to it.

Swift Eagle returned to the Winthrop House and enjoyed a dinner of crisp fried chicken, savory brown gravy, and fresh baked hot biscuits at the long table in the kitchen. He went to the porch where his mother was watching the people in the road.

This was like a fiesta to most of the people knowing these men had killed an innocent man and abducted a little girl much less stolen the horses from the man they killed and his cowboys had been wounded. It was justice and they were in the road celebrating. Star and Calhoun's served chicken and biscuits to the crowd. The kids ran kicking cans and playing up and down the road until late.

Later on Sheriff Henry his deputies along with, Quint, and Swift Eagle removed the bodies and put them in six pine boxes on the wagon, climbed up behind the mules and drove on to boot hill.

It was a good five miles out of town. The men of the town helped bury them. David said a few words of prayer something like if you live by the sword, you die by the sword. Then may God have mercy on their souls. The boxes were lowered into the ground and covered with sand. The hanging completed.

Swift Eagle waited to see his Uncle Brad alone. "Uncle, I am going to the ghost forest and talk with my father, would you wish to come with me? I will be gone not know how many moons."

"Frank Jr. why are you going to stay so long?"

"Me not going to stay only want to talk with father, Tall Brave Man Frank. Me wait for him to come see me."

"Well, sure I would like to go with you if you are going to talk with my brother's spirit, I wish to see him too."

"We go in morning, you bring blanket and gun. Me bring gun, knife and bow, we eat squirrel, rabbit, and fish me cook over fire."

You are not talking like Randy teaching you, Frank, Jr."

"Uncle Brad, me forget."

"Yeah, but me bring salt, me likes salt and bread with me meat, Frank Jr."

Swift Eagle looked at him puzzled. "Why you talk like me Uncle Brad?"

Brad laughed. "Me don't know? You must be contagious."

"What that contagious word mean?"

"Never mind for now, I will tell you later." He laughed again.

Swift Eagle looked at his uncle then said, "Ugh, Uncle Brad, you bring salt, coffee. I bring pot we make coffee have stream for water."

"I will be ready when you say, but tell your mother and the sheriff needs to know so they won't think were are lost and get a posse to try and find us."

"Me tell mother and Sheriff Buck Henry me go see father Tall Brave Man Frank. Uncle Brad go see him with me."

Brad thought you do that Frank Jr. and Sheriff Henry will think we are both looney and got moon shine in our veins. He didn't say anything more Brad knew Sheriff Henry was used to strange things happening with this half-breed nephew of his. He wondered about this camping experience and was actually looking forward to it. I'll be damned if I am going to eat squirrel and rabbit without some salt on it. Coffee made with creek water was okay, without sugar or milk unless the nephew had it with him. He went to his room in the Winthrop House and got his blanket, he knew he would have a beard by the time he returned. His nephew didn't have a beard it was from his mother's side of the family.

So what, he might as well look like a wooley bear after a week or so in the woods. He decided to let Randy and the sheriff know they were just going camping to get away a while after the trial and hanging. They both understood. The sheriff was used to these things, his nephew didn't care. He would have dealt his own kind of justice for what they had done.

Next morning Brad joined Swift Eagle on the porch with his back pack and supplies. They walked to the edge of the woods back of the Winthrop House. Before long he was almost running to keep up with his nephew.

"Hey, there man slow down. I am not used to this you know, I am out of breath."

"Huh, Uncle Brad, not good Indian, he like squaw on trail."

Brad had stopped and sat leaning against a tree. He had worn boots while Frank Jr. had his moccasins and buckskins, his bow over his shoulder and the quiver with the arrows strapped on his back.

"Hey! Uncle Brad, you tenderfoot."

"Will you shut the hell up, I am coming with you ain't I?"

Frank Jr. was laughing out loud and said, "I see my Uncle Brad get pissed off at Swift Eagle."

Brad stood up and took him by the shoulder and slapped his back.

"Come on, Frank Jr., let's get on the trail. If you know where the hell, we're going and how to get back to Black Water."

"We where we go no brother of my father, Tall Brave Man Frank ever go. Uncle not know how to travel in woods like his brother, Tall Brave Man Frank."

"Uh huh, me brother. He had much practice Nephew."

"Aiee Aiee" Swift Eagle raised his head giving the howling sound which was known as the Death Wind.

Brad was astonished he hadn't heard it up close except when they were hunting the six men who kidnapped the little girl as he shot his arrow through the kidnappers shoulder. He ran in and lifted the girl to safety. His nephew, never ceased to amaze him. Frank had quite a son Brad could understand now why his brother was happy here with his new found people.

They stopped in a cleared place beside the creek the water clear and running swiftly, he dropped his blanket, bow and quiver down,, Then sort of dropped down, drinking water from the creek, and splashed his face. Brad knew he had tin cups in his back pack, he took his cup got his drink, he then lay back looking up through the trees at the sun going down over to the west. Brad drew a long breath of fresh pine scented air lying there neither talking.

Suddenly a strong cold wind blew through the trees, ripples glistened along the creek. Brad felt a strange chill come over him. His nephew raised his head, Brad looked and listened, amazed at the sound his nephew made.

"Aiee, Aiee" then was silent as if listening with his eyes closed. Brad thought, I wonder if this is where my brother Frank appears. It was as if Swift Eagle read his thoughts.

"My father is not here yet, He and the braves will come later in the night, I go get food," he disappeared.

It was then Brad thought oh my God what if he doesn't come back, I don't know where the hell I am. He got up and went to the creek, he was surprised to see brim in deep holes, and minnows along the bank. Wild violets and moss fern grew there, too. Wouldn't this be a perfect place to build a home? But where was this place? Brad pulled some branches and stripped the leaves to make the ground under his blanket a little softer, He knew his brother had lived and enjoyed this kind of life. It seemed strange he would have left the comforts of his home in Boston for this life.

Off in the distance he could hear Swift Eagle again.

"Aiee, Aiee."

He guessed it meant he was retuning to their camp. It wasn't long before he heard the bushes and there was his nephew holding two rabbits. He had cleaned them and placed them on the edge of the creek while he built the fire to cook over.

"Uncle Brad, we now have food, me cook rabbit."

As Brad sat watching this young man, he thought, this was as common to him as me drinking a cup of coffee. Swift Eagle arranged two stout green live oak branches into the ground, a limb on the side of the branch he stove into the ground. Then he placed a rabbit on the out reaching branch where it would rest over the coals. The savory smell of the sizzling meat filled the area,

Brad said, "Which one is my dinner, Frank Jr.? I will salt mine."

"You bring salt, Uncle, you salt both." Brad sprinkled salt on each of them as the meat began sizzling over the hot coals. He placed his hands behind his head, leaned back against the live oak tree, and closed his eyes enjoying the scents of warm pine needles, wild flowers, and wet sand by the creek. These fragrances mingled with the fresh air.

By the time night closed in they had finished their rabbit, had a cup of coffee, and Brad was dozing. Another strong breeze raced through the trees, the brush seemed to open and there appeared his brother Frank with a band of Indian braves. Brad gasp, sat up, and speechless.

His nephew said, "Father, I am glad to see you with us."

Frank looked over at his brother.

Brad couldn't believe he was seeing his brother. He finally found his voice. "Frank, I am here with your son, Frank Jr. I am glad to see you."

"Oh, yes, I was watching when you had trouble with your boots, you should have moccasins like Swift Eagle,"

"I will have a pair made when we get back to civilization."

"Father, I thought I could see you and the braves at the trial of the men who stole horses and killed the rancher."

"Yes, Swift Eagle, we stood silently by watching to see justice done."

"I thought we would not have that kind of thing any more."

"Son, as long as there are humans on the earth there will be those kind of men, who want what someone else worked for. Thank goodness for men like Sheriff Buck Henry, blacksmith, Quint, and saloon owner Calhoun. They get the job done."

"Yes, you are right brother, Frank, different justice than Boston. I would say."

"How is your mother getting along now managing the Winthrop House, Swift Eagle?"

"Oh, you know about that father?"

"Yes, of course, but I can't materialize there and talk with her because the dimension I am in is different and doesn't allow it."

Brad then joined the conversation, "Well now, Brother, that explains some of my questions as to how I can see you hear and what you're saying."

"I wanted to see you. Brad. I guess you know our grandparents are also in this dimension, so we are with each other now."

"This was why the holdings they left gave Morning Star and your children the opportunity they now have."

"Say, by the way, Brad, when are you planning to marry again?"

"Frank, I am courting so to speak a lovely woman now. It's nothing serious. I don't know if I will want to marry again."

"Well, give yourself time and now my grown son how about you? Have you given thought to marriage?"

"No, father I haven't. Chief Lone Wolf's granddaughter, Red Wing was looking at me when we lived in camp but she is shy."

"Go back and see her, Son. She has not been taken in marriage yet."

"Is this why you wanted me to come here, Father?"

"One of the reasons, but I also wanted to see my brother and how he liked our way of life in the forest."

"I hear you, Frank. You were always the venturesome one of us. I would never have been here except for you and my special sister-in-law, nephew, and niece. I have a sister I never had."

"Tell mother and dad about being here. You know she used to have séances and talk with the departed."

"Yes, Frank, I will write her and let her know you and her parents are all right and together."

Before Swift Eagle could say what he started to they disappeared.

"Will we go back tomorrow, Frank, Jr?" Brad asked him.

"No, Uncle Brad, I stay two days, you wait, is good here, many rabbit, plenty squirrel, and you got salt and plenty coffee. Me know how to find food and find the way home from forest."

"I cannot believe you put that sentence together."

"You wish me talk like white man, Uncle Brad?"

"Hey, forget it. I just was surprised."

"Ha, Uncle is pissed at Swift Eagle again."

Brad ignored the remark. He laid back down on his blanket and fell asleep.

Swift Eagle kept the fire burning at night to keep wolves and bear away. He remained awake all night thinking his father might return. He thought of the camp and Red Wing. He would ask her grandfather if he thought Red Wing would be his squaw. He hadn't gotten around to it though and things changed after he met his father's brother, Uncle Brad. He would take a trip and see if she had married.

He had some quail over the coals for their breakfast when his uncle awakened. The coffee was boiling, it smelled good.

Brad went to the creek washed his face and dried it on his shirt tail. This was new for him. What would his mother say? He smiled thinking about it. Frank Jr. gave him a quail on a stick, he poured a cup of coffee, then sat enjoying his breakfast.

The morning was nice, although it looked like would rain. He guessed he would have to get used to it, if he were to be an outdoors man.

They stayed two more days, then started back to Black Water. Brad watched carefully how his nephew found the way. He would look at the tree tops and the bark on them then move one-way or the other. One thing sure, Brad could never find the way back to the creek unless he blazed those trees.

•••••

When he got to his room he called to Morning Star.

"Yes, Brad, what is it?"

"I want to take a bath if no one else has it please."

"I will heat the water for you and call when it is ready."

He was so glad to get cleaned up, shaved and clean clothes, he thought on what Frank said about marriage. He knew Miss Webster seemed interested, but he wasn't sure about himself. He decided to ask her to go riding again after Sunday services. He would tell her of his marriage, so she would know how it was with him. He wondered if she had been married, jilted, or just didn't have any interest in marriage. He would find out Sunday.

Swift Eagle told Morning Star about the visit with her husband, Frank. She was happy to know he sort of watched over her though unseen. He also told her he was going to visit the camp asking if she would like to come along. He would get a horse and buggy.

"No, Swift Eagle, my home is here now. You may tell Chief Lone Wolf I would be happy if you and his granddaughter were to marry."

"Mother, I am not sure if she is another brave's squaw by now. Father wanted me to see her. I will get one of Quint's horses and be gone a week."

He bathed, dressed in clean buckskins and moccasins. He packed a small satchel with change of clothing. He was on the way and reached Chief Lone Wolf's camp by dusk. Chief Lone Wolf was sitting by his fire, and glad to see Swift Eagle. He could see Red Wing peek out the door of her parents' teepee. He waved to her.

That night Lone Wolf had venison stew and corn pone. Swift Eagle enjoyed the supper, and was invited to sleep in Chief Lone Wolf's teepee. He wanted to sleep outside near the fire. Red Wing came over to see him while he was eating. She sat beside him, asking about his two sisters. He told her they had different names now Sylvia, Whitney, and Star. She thought they were all right. He asked Red Wing if she wanted to be a squaw of Swift Eagle.

"I have always loved you Swift Eagle since we small children. I would be your squaw. You must ask my grandfather."

Swift Eagle took her hand and pressed it to his heart. "I will take care of Red Wing forever."

The two then went to Chief Lone Wolf at hist eepee.

"Come, my children, sit with me." The two joined him by his fire.

"Chief Lone Wolf, me ask if you give Red Wing as my squaw?"

The old chief sat silently puffing his pipe, looking into the embers of his fire. The couple sat silent waiting for his reply. He turned and looked at his granddaughter, saying, "My granddaughter, Red Wing, if you be Swift Eagle squaw then Red Wing leave, and live with him at, the Black Water camp. You must be sure you would be happy there away from your people."

She turned to Swift Eagle and said, "If I go with you, Swift Eage , will I be free to come back here to see my people?"

All this time her mother and father sat a little behind Chief Lone Wolf, listening to the conversation. Now Swift Eagle looked to them, "Tall Bear and Little Faun, I would like to be your son if you would have me as Red Wing, her brave and man of her teepee. I would want you happy if I take her to my camp as my squaw."

Everyone was quiet thinking about what he had said. Tall Bear then replied, "Swift Eagle, you will be my son."

Little Faun, smiled at her daughter and Swift Eagle. Chief Lone Wolf then stood and said

"We will have the ceremony, dance, and food tomorrow. You will be brave and squaw. I will say the words and our camp will dance in joy together at your council."

Red wing smiled at Swift Eagle and reached over shyly kissing his cheek. They joined her parents at their teepee and sat. Swift Eagle with his arm around Red Wing.

She went in with her parents for the night. Swift Eagle spread his blanket behind their teepee and settled down for the remainder of the night. A strong wind blew through the trees, he wondered if his father was watching out there looking up at the stars he drifted to sleep.

A t dawn the camp was busy preparing for the wedding celebration feast and ceremony. The braves had been given
sleigh bells by Red Beard knowing they would enjoy their
dancing along with the drums, chants, and the bells would
add to their joy.

Swift Eagle went to the creek, washed, and came back
to eat breakfast with Red Wing and her parents. Little Faun
cooked grits, fried salt pork, biscuits, gravy, and coffee with
cream and sugar. The trading post was always supplied now
since Brad Winthrop had come into their lives. The wild black
berry jam was delicious on the hot biscuits with the coffee.
They sat enjoying their togetherness. When they finished
Swift Eagle helped the braves with the fire and the spit to roast
the venison. There would be more food, rabbit and wild hog
roasted. The elders sent runners to invite the family at Black
Water and Red Beard to join them in the celebration.

Swift Eagle wondered if he would come to share their marriage. He wished that his Uncle Brad would be there. The runners had already gone to Black Water. Chief Lone Wolf would wait for his family to arrive. The camp was enjoying the smell of the meat cooking and sweet potatoes roasting in the coals.

Unknown to him, his mother, Morning Star had asked Brad to get a wagon and the girls and friends would be there with them on the joyful occasion. The second day passed.

They were just starting the dance around the large fire in the center of the tents as the group from Black Water pulled into the camp. The braves stopped and ran to greet their guests and family. Morning Star was greeted royally as was Brad Winthrop, Red Beard now felt more at ease seeing a fellow white man there with him.

The teachers Julie and Randy joined them. It was really a camp filled with well-wishers and friends. They were given fresh water, and soon joined the braves in the ceremonial dance with bells ringing, chanting, and drums beating. What a special group sharing together their joy and happiness. Brad was more or less speechless, in awe, never in his wildest dreams thinking of such a wedding celebration. One, thing it was different from his wedding years ago. He was really enjoying this one. He hoped his brother, Frank, was out there watching his son's wedding.

When the dancing quieted down, Chief Lone Wolf came to the center of the camp, motioned the couple to join him beside the fire. Red Wing was beautiful with beaded head band, moccasins, and buckskin dress. Chief Lone Wolf was regal in full feather head dress, special buckskin trappings. The Chief stood in the center, he raised his hand with the ceremonial wand of feathers, bells, and beads, chanting the ceremony handed down through the ages. He emphasized each sentence with the wand to be sure it was sacred. Brad and the others felt honored to be present at this sacred ritual for the couple. Even the Native American college graduate school teacher Randy Swain, had never seen his ancestors perform this ritual. He only had heard about it from the missionaries before he was adopted by the English couple. He felt humble being there.

Everyone enjoyed the food, and festivities. Brad and Morning Star, decided to start back to Black Water knowing it would be way into the night and next day before they would get home. They stocked enough water and food to last them, along with hay and grain for the horses. The branch ran along the woods road, so the horses could have water. Everyone was sleeping as they started along the trail home. Swift Eagle and Red Wing joined them behind on horseback. Her father gave her his favorite mare as her wedding gift. She was riding it along beside Swift Eagle. They would spend their honeymoon in the forest after they arrived at Black Water. He planned to take her to the ghost forest where his father, Tall Brave Man Frank, would come to bless them. He had built his own house before traveling into the forest. The last time. His uncle had advised him to purchase as much land as his eye could see now he had wampum. They could plant apple trees, peach trees, and build houses to sell or rent to others who would settle in Black Water. When they got home Morning Star prepared a lovely dinner for every one at the Winthrop House.

Then Red Wig went to his home as his squaw. Red Wing had been told the facts of life by her mother and many of her girlfriends were married. They shared their inner most secrets with her, laughing and giggling like silly girls. Many of them had babies the first year. Their papoose strapped to their back as they went about their daily chores while their braves hunted for food and furs to sell at the Trading Post.

Swift Eagle gently cradled Red Wing in his arms brushed her hair back from her lovely face he kissed her telling her, "Me happy you be my wife."

Red Wing put her arms around his neck and kissed him. He held her tenderly making love to her. She was happy now being Swift Eagle's squaw. They would be together for ever.

Next morning, they went to the hotel and had breakfast with the others. She met the doctors and was glad to be with Silver Wing and White Cloud again. They showed her the school room and where they had gone to learn to write and read like the white man. Red Wing wanted to learn how to read and write.

Red Wing helped around the hotel while Swift Eagle was busy talking with his Uncle Brad about building some homes for his tribesmen and giving them a place to work and earn money. Instead of living at the Trading Post unless they really wished to. Brad knew the railroad would be coming this way soon. If they had something the people outside really wanted and needed they could set up a plant to build or manufacture the needed items. It sounded good to Swift Eagle to see his people independent of the government again in their lives to be free. He also knew they needed food and the tribesmen could learn to farm and ship the vegetables or perhaps have a canning plant. He wanted to see what his Grandfather Winthrop had to say about all of this. But, first he wanted to take his bride to meet his father, Tall Brave Man Frank. He would do this next week.

Red Wing remembered his father before he was killed by the renegade although she was just a little girl. She had heard of the ghost people who lived deep in the forest and wondered about meeting them.

28

Swift Eagle made preparations for them to take the trip into the deep forest. He packed dry hides, he would cut the poles for their teepee when they got to the camp. The creek would have water for coffee corn pone, bathing and other needs. He, of course, armed himself with bow, arrows, his special knife, and now rifle. They had some salt pork flour, hog fat just enough for a few days away from the hotel.

Red Wing had a small satchel with a few clean things to change into while she was there and her moccasins. She had her blanket in a bag on her back with the other things. They were up early this Monday morning, had some breakfast, and quickly went behind Winthrop House to where the forest began. Swift Eagle found the path he and his Uncle Brad had traveled, it would take them to the ghost forest. Red Wing walked behind Swift Eagle as was their custom. He went at a swift pace and it was sort of a challenge for her to keep up with him until he realized she wasn't used to the pace he was setting. He stopped and waited for her to catch up to him.

"Red Wing, me forget you not used to this."

She came and sat beside him. "I need to wait and get my wind back. Swift Eagle, you walk too fast for me."

"Come a little way and we stay the night near a creek. Me make coffee, we eat, and stay until morning. Then we to ghost forest."

They went on and soon came to the creek. Red Wing quickly went to wash her face, laid down drinking from the clear fresh water. She was glad they would rest now for the night. She was tired from the day's journey through the heavy forest and her feet too were blistered from the fast pace they had been going. She soaked her feet in the creek down from the camp, then spread her blanket by Swift Eagle.

"Me go hunt food." he returned shortly with several partridge, she helped clean them and had them roasting over the coals with two rolls of corn pone. The sat eating, enjoying their solitude, and the roasted meat. After eating the lay by the large fire. Red Wing wrapped in his arms for the night.

A hoot owl called out, "Whoo, whoo" while it looked down keeping watch over them, and hoped for a rabbit or something left by the fire. Another hoot owl echoed away off in the distance answered the call, "Whoo, whoo."

The crescent of the new moon shone through the leaves of the tall live oak trees. The hoot owl sat blinking its eyes in the glare from the fire, a rabbit hearing the owl, scurried through the brush to hide.

Red Wing snuggled close to Swift eagle contented in his blanket and arms. He smiled down at her and kissed her tenderly. He loved Red Wing since they were children. She called him her brave at an early age. He of course tried to show off for her by hunting, bringing her birds and a rabbit he caught with his first bow and arrow.

Early next morning, Swift Eagle carefully went to a deep place in the creek where there was brim, he quickly speared four of them, wrapped them in palmetto leaves, and set them to bake in the coals. Red Wing awakened, and they enjoyed breakfast of corn pone bread from his back pack. They started on to the ghost forest, where they would meet his father.

The sun was sinking when they arrived at the river, fog hung like a curtain over everything. Swift Eagle built a fire and set poles to stretch the hides over for the night here. The fog was very thick and cold. Soon he could hear drums from across the river. They walked to the edge of the river and watched as his father, Brave Tal Man Frank, raised his hand to hail them as he approached.

"Swift Eagle, my son I am happy you come and bring squaw with you. I am happy to see you little, Red Wing."

"Father Frank, me happy to see you and know you, too."

"Swift Eagle, I hear from others your mother Morning Star is happy at Black Water away from the tribe."

"Yes, Father, we are what is called rich now from great grandfather. We buy hotel for mother, we happy there."

"Father Frank, me will learn to write and read as white father of my husband, me go at the school now."

"It is good, Red Wing. I am happy to know this. I welcome you as my daughter."

"We will stay tonight, Father, and go home in the morning."

"Be safe my son. I will talk with you when you leave." Frank vanished into the curtain fog mist. The drums beat softly in the distance.

They had dry corn pone and settled down for the night. She curled closely in his arms and slept soundly until day light. They left the poles and said farewell to Father Frank then began the trek through the ghost forest. The sun was setting when they came to the camp where they had stayed two nights ago. He built the fire up caught two rabbits, roasted them, and soon after eating were asleep. The fire burning brightly until dawn. Swift Eagle had brim baked, and fresh coffee when Red Wing awakened. After eating and seeing the fire safely out, they started on the trail home.

Sunset found them out of the forest and on the path to their hotel. Morning Star greeted them happy they were home safe.

Her new daughter asked, "Mother Star, me want hot bath, if is all right?"

"Yes, my daughter, I have hot water in tub for you." She went and poured the water from the wood reservoir into the large tin tub, cooled it, and left Red Wing there. Red Wing was glad to be home she planned to soak in hot bath, have something to eat, sleep in her own house, and bed tonight on the soft cotton mattress.

Morning Star had beef stew and hot biscuits for dinner. Red Wing thought she had never eaten anything as delicious. The regular boarders went to the living room as did Julie, Randy, and Brad. Whitney and Sylvia helped do the dishes and were surprised to hear music coming from the living room. The curiosity got the best of them, Randy was at the piano. Julie was singing along to the music. The girls were surprised. They knew Mrs. Brooks played at church on Sundays. They went in to listen.

Red Wing and Frank Jr. finished eating. He told his mother about their visit with his father Frank and he was glad they were happy here. She smiled remembering the tall white man she had married and had children with. Red Wing and Frank Jr. got up to go home. Morning Star walked with them to the front porch and watched them as they walked to the house Brad and the others had built. Tomorrow was another day.

29

Red Wing was happy to go to the school house this morning. Swift Eagle had been learning to write and to read a little. She was anxious to read. Julie and Randy had about ten students entering school for the first time. They divided them the girls were in Julie's room and boys in Randy's. They would change classes to get used to each teacher. Red Wing was excited when called to hand out the pencils with another girl who gave each student a new spelling tablet. They sat quietly waiting to find out what to do next. The room had been divided with lumber shipped in by mule and wagon from the nearest saw mill. It gave more privacy and less noise for each class.

Julie began, "Ladies, open your tablets and on the top of each page you will see what is called an alphabet. It is letters you will learn so you can read and write. I will name them and you then say them with me."

The students were eager to learn. Strong Bow listened outside the window. He knew Silvia wanted him to learn to read and write. He was embarrassed and shy about it.

So began Red Wing's first day of school. She now was known as Ruth Red Wing Winthrop. She learned to write and spell her name. That evening, as they all sat eating supper Morning Star asked Red Wing if she could read her name yet.

"Mother Star, Ruth my name now Ruth Winthrop." She spelled each letter clear and loud.

"Wow! That's great, Ruth. I am proud of you," Brad told her.

Swift Eagle didn't say anything just went on eating his beans and rice. He had already been learning to read, write, and was speaking very good English, Brad thought. He knew his mother and dad would be proud when he wrote them about it.

After eating they went to the living room the girls, as usual helped put things away and wash dishes, then joined the others. Everyone enjoyed listening to Dr. Young play the piano. Julie often sang along.

Tonight the piano was playing itself. Dr. Young looked around at the amazed faces. "This is called a player piano. It makes music and has pedals you can push so it plays by itself."

The others sat waiting, not saying anything. He found some rolls in the piano bench and then put a roll in the front of the old upright. He started pedaling.

It was pretty Star thought.

The tune was the Blue Danube. When it finished he rewound the roll and closed the front of the piano. He stood up and then everyone wanted him to pedal more.

"This was a different kind of music," Swift Eagle went to it and lifted the top he pushed the keys and heard the clink of the hammers against the strings. There weren't bells with the drums.

Dr. Young realized they had much to learn. It was a joy to be able to help them learn the white man's ways. Although they had more honesty and honor than the white man ever had. He thought it would be an opportunity to teach piano lessons along with being a physician in Black Water. It would teach him many different things about humans.

• • • • •

Time went by, the bank was established, Red Wing bore a son to Swift Eagle, and Star was delighted at her first grandchild. They named him Little Eagle Winn. Short for Winthrop. Red Wing talked to her mother-in-law about Frank Jr.

"Mother Star, he is having dreams at night about my grandfather, Lone Wolf."

"What do you mean, Red Wing?"

"He talks in his sleep saying. I am coming Lone Wolf. I will help you."

"I will see him, Red Wing, and find out if I can what is the trouble."

Red Wing was now helping at the school as the helper in the kindergarten class. They had five new little people there now.

Later in the afternoon when Frank Jr. came by the hotel he said, "Mother, I must talk with you about something."

"Yes, Son, what is troubling you?"

"I am hearing Lone Wolf calling me for help. I must go to him and help him."

"How is it you hear him call you?"

"In my mind I see him lying on the ground by his cold camp fire, crawling, and calling me. I will go when I pack my bow, arrows, knife, and rifle. I want you to watch my wife and son. Keep them safe until I return."

He then told his Uncle Brad to watch over his mother, his wife, and son. Brad didn't understand his nephew's reasoning but promised to watch over them until he returned.

He went to his home and told Ruth he must go to Lone Wolf's camp.

"I will go with you, my husband, and see my mother and father."

"No! You stay with Mother Star until I return," he quickly packed his things, dressed in buckskins, and moccasins. He picked up Winn, hugged him, placed him back in his crib, hugged Ruth, and was gone. He went to Quint's to get his horse and ride on to Lone Wolf's camp where he had been born.

Quint knowing something was not as it should be decided to go with him. They put the horses into an easy canter. They would arrive by night fall.

30

Swift Eagle and Quint could hear Lone Wolf's call as they approached the camp. It was deserted and no fires burned. This was unusual they always kept the fires burning day and night. They quickly rode into the camp jumped down from their horses. They could see bodies lying on the ground by the cold fires. Swift Eagle rushed to Chief Lone Wolf.

"Thank you, Swift Eagle. You heard my call. See to my daughter, Faun and her husband, Tall Bear. They need help."

Quint was kneeling by Little Faun and Tall Bear. They were semi-conscious and had been beaten severely. Swift Eagle wondered why anyone would want to hurt either of them or the old Chief Lone Wolf. He wanted to find who did this.

"Chief Lone Wolf, what happened? Who did to you?"

"Yes, water please, we need water," The men quickly found a couple of cups and ran to the creek for water. Holding the cup and their heads up, the three sipped water graciously. They were dried out and beaten horribly.

"Tell me, Chief Lone Wolf, who did this?"

"The men hunt for you, Swift Eagle. They beat Red Beard to make him tell where the camp is. They come here to find Swift Eagle. Him not tell you went to live in Black Water."

"Me be happy for him to find, Swift Eagle. Me help him find me."

Swift Eagle quickly went to the creek again and gave them more water. He and Quint built the teepee and cleansed their wounds finding grass and moss to lay blankets over for a bed. They moved the three there.

Chief Lone Wolf told Swift Eagle, the thugs had slipped in and caught Tall Bear off guard, hit him over the head, then beat him as another thug beat Chief Lone Wolf. He turned and hit Little Faun with his rifle her unconscious. They were caught off guard, never thinking anyone would want to kill them.

"Me go to Trading Post, see Red Beard if he lives. We bring food. Be back soon." He and Quint left running. They cautiously approached the trading post. Red Beard was lying on the floor, gasping for breath and barely alive. They quickly gave him fresh water and lifted him onto his bed. Quint knew he had whiskey in his trunk. He found it and gave him some to stimulate his heart. His breathing became steady and he glanced up at them.

"Swift Eagle, you are here. Thank Thunder God."

"Red Beard, what happened? Who did this to you?"

"These men are relatives of the man who kill you father, Tall Brave Man Frank. They wish to kill you and avenge their uncle."

"I will take care of them. Where did they go, Red Beard? How long ago?"

"They were going on path to Black Water. You must have seen them on your way here," he fell back unconscious again. Swift Eagle looked over at Quint.

"Yes," Quint replied, "remember two men passed us and never stopped? Just ran on past us."

"Yes, I hope Sheriff Henry will notice when they ride in and guard my mother and family until we return. Now I must care for these here." He made a fire in the stove. There was some meat in the smoke house. He cooked stew. Red Beard regained consciousness, Quint wiped Red Beard's face and hands. He was feeling better and able to sit up. They gave him a bowl of stew. He was trembling trying to hold the bowl and feed him.

"Red Beard, we take food to Chief Lone Wolf, his son, and daughter they very weak. We take all with us to Black Water. No one left at trading post now. Too much alone we have things to do at Black Water. You can help there."

"Yes, Swift Eagle, I will go with you and Quint." He fell back on his bed unconscious again. There was nothing else to do for him. They needed to see to the others.

Rushing back to the camp with food and water to care for the chief, his son, and daughter. They were weak, but felt stronger after eating .Quint had the whiskey and had given each a shot of whiskey to stimulate their heart.

Swift Eagle said, "Chief Lone Wolf, me know the renegade go to Black Water to find me. We pass on road."

"Swift Eagle, my son you must hurry and go care for your people in Black Water."

"Yes, my chief, we take you, Little Faun, Tall Bear, and Red Beard in wagon with us to Black Water. Is no one left at Indian camp. We take you with your own people, Chief Lone Wolf."

Quint was busy hitching the horses to the wagon. It would be a slow, rough ride, but at least it was better than having them on a travois behind the horses. They padded the wagon bed with the gray Spanish moss which hung from the giant oak trees and covered it with blankets. Swift Eagle gently lifted his mother-in-law, Little Faun onto the wagon and helped Tall Bear up. Quint helped Chief Lone Wolf. He would lay beneath the driver's seat with a little shade. Quint filled pottery jugs with fresh water from the flowing well at the post. There was dried meat in the smoke house. He wrapped it and placed it under the wagon seat out of the sun. It would take at least two days on the road, unless they drove nights.

Before Swift Eagle climbed on the wagon he went to the burned out camp fire and raised his head. "Ayee, ayee, Great Spirit help me find men who did this."

Chief Lone Wolf, hadn't heard this sound for many moons. Swift Eagle's Death Wind sounded throughout the woodland. A strong wind blew through the forest whipping the ashes around in a whirl wind. A gray mist appeared, the spirit of his father and the tribe appeared in the gray mist, the whisper came to them. His father Tall Brave Man Frank spoke out from the mist, "Chief Lone Wolf, we go with you. Our elders wish to see justice done again for the renegade relatives of man who killed me. I want them to be brought to justice. They tried to kill Chief Lone Wolf, his son and daughter who survived. Red Beard wouldn't tell them where you were, Swift Eagle, so they tried to beat him to death. The Great Thunder Bird Spirit God will not let it go unpunished. We are here to see you safely home and see them put in prison."

Swift Eagle thought they not see prison, me find first. His father knew if his son caught them he would render his own justice.

The gray mist gradually faded away but a whisper of voices were still heard and drums beating in the distance.

Quint knew the two men would be dealt with in his friend's own style.

Swift Eagle thought to himself, ugh they not need prison when me find them. Me take care of like when he kill my father. He knew the law now would try to defend these men, but he also knew he had a way of getting around the law and it would look as an accident. Of course, they could just ride off and disappear. Their horses found without riders and not know where they disappeared. The horses were army anyway and would eventually find their way back to the fort if these two were to get lost in the forest.

These thoughts ran through Swift Eagle's mind as they rode along with their family in the wagon bed, still suffering from the beating the rogues gave. They tried to kill them, but thanks to the Great Thunder Bird Spirit God, they survived. Well Swift Eagle thought I will take care of it. First, I must know my son, wife, mother and sisters are safe. He also knew Sheriff Buck Henry would be keeping a close watch on these new comers riding the army horses into town.

As night closed in, the men pulled the wagon off the woods road and made camp, for the night. Little Faun asked Swift Eagle to help her to the bushes where she could relieve herself, He waited a distance from her and when she called to him. He carried her back to the wagon. He helped Chief Lone Wolf, too so they would be comfortable for now. He noticed Red Beard was unconscious yet breathing normally. They let him be for now. Quint built a fire and they roasted several rabbits. After eating and seeing their passengers were alright. Quint raised Red Beard and gave him water with a bit of whiskey. He coughed opened his eyes and looked up at them.

"Aye there. Lad. Thank ye. I am most grateful," he lay back down. The men decided to get back on the trail and not waste any time. They traveled the balance of the night and next day stopping only for the passengers to relieve themselves. Swift Eagle helped Little Faun down from the wagon and a distance from it. Then returned to the wagon and waited at the wagon until she called for him. The men didn't have any problem, were ready to get back in the wagon, and on the trail. They gave the passengers cold broth from the stew in the jug they had filled before leaving the camp.

Quint thought it was because of the great Thunder Bird Spirit God they still lived. They went on over the bumpy road in silence.

Finally they arrived in Black Water the following night. They carried Little Faun into the hotel. Chief Lone Wolf was able to walk with Quint's assistance. Tall Bear had regained his strength now and walked without help. Red Beard was in and out of consciousness, two of them had to hold him on each side and he was put in a room next to the doctors' office. Star was glad to see them. She immediately settled Little Faun in a room near the kitchen and Tall Bear with her. Star had an extra room near the clinic, Red Beard and Chief Lone Wolf were there for the balance of the night. The doctors hearing them come in were ready to care for their wounds and see them comfortable. Red Beard had a concussion and lapsed into unconsciousness. He had taken the worst of it.

Swift Eagle cautioned the doctors not to mention to anyone about the new patients. He never realized they had a sworn oath not to talk about their patients. After seeing them settled in he ran to the Sheriff's office. He had a room in the back and was sleeping. Quint went with him.

Swift Eagle pounded on the door. "Sheriff! Sheriff! Wake up! It's Frank Winthrop, Jr. we need talk to you now."

Sheriff Henry slowly opened the door of the jail. "What is it Frank? What's the matter?" He was rubbing his eyes trying to wake up. "You and Quint, come in and let's fix some coffee then we can talk."

They followed the sheriff in taking seats near his desk, while he stoked the fire and put the coffee pot on to boil. He placed tin cups on the desk, settled in his chair, and leaned back. "All right now what's goin' on?"

"Sheriff, we look for two strangers. Did they come in town?"

"Well, yes, they are staying at the Winthrop Hotel."

"What! They be ones who try to kill Chief Lone Wolf, Little Faun, Tall Bear, and Red Beard. We go to hotel now."

"What are you talking about, Frank? They just only got here two days ago while you were away?"

"Me know, Sheriff, me have Chief Lone Wolf, daughter, son, and Red Beard in hotel. They in danger from these men now. Red Beard near beat to death. He unconscious have hole in head from them."

Swift Eagle jumped up and ran toward the hotel, Quint right with him, The sheriff grabbed his pants, his hat, and gun belt, made sure his 45 was loaded, strapped it on, and ran behind them toward the hotel.

Quint waited on the porch. There was nothing more he could do now.

Frank, Jr. silently went to his mother's room and told her the strangers were the ones who tried to kill Chief Lone Wolf and the others. "They must not know they are here in the hotel."

Star knew when the strangers came in on the army horses something wasn't as it should be. Her son had good reason to go see to his family at the camp. She fed the men and acted as if she knew nothing when they asked about a half breed Indian, knowing her son was in danger. She quickly got up, dressed, went to the kitchen to brew coffee. She heard the sheriff and Quint talking with her son. She sat silent, listening.

Swift Eagle motioned the sheriff and Quint, to come outside. They waited on the porch. In whispers, they told Sheriff Henry what had happened to their friends at Red Beards Dusty Road trading post and Lone Wolf's camp.

"Quint and me bring the unconscious, Scotsman with us. If we leave him there he die. Already left for dead.

"I will put them in jail now."

"No, Sheriff Henry, me want to catch them away from here. The soldiers from the fort will take then to fort and they set free. No justice for Red Beard, my Chief, or family. Swift Eagle want them not do it again. The one kill my father, he no do it again."

"They want to kill me. I help them find me, Sheriff."

"Oh, now I see, all right, Frank. But you remember one thing, you and me, we never had this conversation. I never heard anything about it."

"Ugh, me know, Sheriff. They look for Swift Eagle now they find."

Swift Eagle ran to his home to see his son and wife. They were sleeping. He silently went to the bedside and bent down to kiss Red Wing on the cheek. Startled she raised up, he put his hand over her mouth so she wouldn't scream and waken his son.

"Me have Little Faun and Chief Lone Wolf at Winthrop House." She got up, they went to the kitchen, he sat, and told her what had happened at the camp and Red Beard's trading post. He explained her mother, father, and grandfather were at the hotel as were the men who beat them. He must lure them away.

She wanted to go see her mother and father. He told her it best to stay quiet now.

Swift Eagle went back to the jail to talk with Sheriff Henry. The sheriff now had the coffee ready. They sat to discuss what to do about the strangers at the hotel.

They had been questioned by the sheriff when they first rode into town. They told him they were looking for a half breed Indian here. He told them there was more than one such person in Black Water and asked his name. They had replied it had something to do with a sound this half breed made like a death wind. Sheriff immediately knew it was Swift Eagle they referred to. He never said anything. He wondered why they wanted to see him

"Sheriff Henry, I have plan, go to teepee at forest by Ghost River, and build fire. You tell men Indian camp at forest in tee-pee, then you shut mouth. Sheriff understand?"

"I understand, go. I will see them early this morning. If they go to forest they will find the half breed Indian with the death wind." He turned to put the coffee pot back on the stove. He started to speak turned and Swift Eagle was gone.

He would catch the two rouges and see justice was meted out to them as it was to their relative who killed his father. He told his mother to keep the chief, his daughter, and son safe from these men. The sheriff would be there soon to tell where Swift Eagle was camped.

Star knew her son planned to catch the two men and give them what they wanted his kind of justice. Still she was frightened for her son.

The next morning Sheriff Henry knocked on the door of the hotel, Star came and let him. He went upstairs where the two men were still sleeping and knocked on their door.

H ey Fellas, I just found where the half-breed is.

They came to the door pulling on their pants, "You know where he is, Sheriff?"

"Yes, I saw his fire last night. He has a camp outside of town near the Black Water Forest. If you hurry you will catch him before he goes hunting."

Years had passed since his father was murdered. He administered his own brand of revenge against the killer of his father. Now these ignorant cousins wanted to show off and kill a half-breed, so they could brag about it to the relatives back home. Well, they would find the half-breed.

Swift Eagle was standing around the fire, he saw them coming on horseback. He quickly put out the fire and immediately started running into the dense forest as though he was afraid of them, knowing they would try to follow him. As they trampled the brush the horses became entangled in vines growing there. The two started following him on foot leaving the horses.

Swift Eagle thought, *just what I wanted. Now you two keep following me. There is* a pond with interesting water. Now the army knows me have own justice not leave trail.

Noon approached he could see they were tiring, but he showed himself just enough for them to take a shot at him. Then hurried on toward the quick sand pond. As they neared the pond. He faked as if he were crawling to get a drink of water. They ran quickly to the quick sand pond and dived in before they knew what had happened.

Swift Eagle raised his head "Aieee, Aiee."

They now knew what the Death Wind sound was.

"Aiee Aiee, Thunder Spirit God."

The strong wind blew through, bending the trees in the forest, the gray mist filled the trees. He stood a moment, they were shouting, "Help please. We're sorry, please help."

He ran back the way they came hearing their cries, "Help! Help! We need help! Come help!"

"Ugh, you need much help. Red Beard also needed much help, you left him to die."

He continued running and soon came to the ghost forest, the gray mist settled in the forest.

The spirit ghosts of the tribesmen were there with his father, Tall Brave Man Frank.

"Good hunting Swift Eagle, the Great Thunder Bird Spirit is well pleased."

The wind blew fiercely, hail, and rain poured in torrents. Large hail stone covered the forest ground. Swift Eagle sheltered under an old live oak tree, when the storm passed he ran on toward the Black Water forest. He ran all night to his Teepee and camp.

He found the two army horses still tangled in vines, led them to the clearing, and gave them a slap on the rump. They started running toward the Black Water settlement and on to the army post the McClellan saddles still strapped to their back.

Quint looked up as they ran past his shop headed down the woods road toward the fort. No one knew what happened to the riders. Swift Eagle was at his camp, folded his teepee, scattered the ash remains, covered it with moss, and branches then started toward the village He could take the trail to the pond and be back in two days. He was satisfied. Justice had been done for the near death beatings Red Beard and the others had endured, when they left thinking the Indians and Scotsman dead. No one would know what had happened to them. The Great Thunder Bird Spirit God has ways of knowing when evil like this happens. After clearing the area he ran on toward home.

He broke the poles of the teepee and burned them in his wood stove. He knew now his son and wife would be at the hotel safe with Star. He changed into jeans, western shirt, and boots. He put his moccasins and his buckskins in his blanket, stored them in the closet, then hurried to the hotel. They were eating supper when he came in.

"You're just in time for supper, come Frank and eat with us," Star said getting up from the table. The girls and others looked up and nodded to him.

"Me want bath, Mother, then me eat."

Ruth quickly got up from the table and carried hot water from the reservoir in the wood stove to the tin tub in the back room. She filled cold water from the pump.

He thought, *all of his life he washed in the creek which ran near the camp where they lived long time ago. Now me takes bath in tin tub.*

No one ask any questions, when he came to the table. "Why Red Beard not eat now?"

Doctor Jones answered. "Red Beard is not able to come yet. He is still hurt very bad."

"Ugh, him get better me hunt, bring deer meat. Him get well."

He knew to bring venison as he was hunting those days he was gone, according to Sheriff Henry.

Frank knew he lapsed back into his ignorant speech when it was needed and this was that time. He had learned to read and write. Mr. Shufro helped keeping the bank books in order.

Brad was glad they had his help and his money invested with them. Brad had learned not to ask any questions about where Frank, Jr had gone especially when he learned of the injuries to Red Beard and the Indian relatives of Ruth.

Red Beard, was still unable to stand or come to the table to eat. Dr. Young said he had a concussion, whatever it was and must stay in bed for now. The doctor did have him get up and stand walk a short distance in the room. The girls learned to take vital signs like blood pressure, heart beat, and temperature. . They were studying to be nursing assistants and took turns feeding Red Beard and dressing the knife wounds. His personal bath was done by the doctors.

Chief Lone Wolf was at the table with the others. Everyone was glad to see him.

32

They had retired when Frank Jr, finished bathing and came to the table. He had killed a deer on his way back and cleaned it leaving it at the smoke house where his mother would make a delicious venison stew. Mother Star had biscuits. He sat alone satisfied with his week's work and ready to get back to his bank and see how it was doing.

The three went home this evening. Little Eagle riding on his dad's shoulders. He knew there would be army soldiers here once the horses got back to the fort. They would be asking if anyone knew anything of the two men.

Sheriff Henry only knew he directed them to the trail in the forest where they might find a man they were looking for. The sheriff was not asking Frank, Jr any questions. Everyone else knew he had gone to hunt venison. Star knew her son and he wouldn't let this atrocity go unpunished. She didn't ask him anything and the others were glad to have venison for a change.

Things went along in Black Water as usual for about three months. The army sent soldiers from Fort McKinley to ask about the two missing men who had been going to Red Beards Dusty Road Trading Post. They were surprised when they found Red Beard had closed the Trading Post leaving a note he was moving to Black Water. They found Red Beard working in the grocery store. He was not surprised to see them and knew them. He told them the two men had asked him about the Squaw Man who was killed by the Fur Trappers. They were looking for the man's half-breed son.

"Yes, I told them the Indians had moved away. They wanted to know if I knew where they moved.

"Well, Red Beard. did you tell them where the Indians moved?"

"What I told them was the closest town was Black Water. I didn't know if they went here or not. Why, Sergeant, is there something wrong?" Red Beard ask them.

"We don't know. The horses they took from the fort came in about two weeks ago dragging the reins, still saddled, and could barely stand. They were starved with the lack of feed and bit still in their mouths."

"Goodness what could have happened, Sergeant?"

"It's why we're here. To see if we can get any idea of where they are."

"I closed the store right after they left, Sergeant and my friend, Quint. from Black Water came and helped me pack up and move."

"Where do we find this feller Quint?"

"Oh, he is a blacksmith. He has his corral and stable over back of the sheriff's office and jail."

"Come out to the road and point us in that direction."

"Goodness men you surely couldn't get lost in this small town."

He walked to the door with them, stood on the porch, and pointed the direction of the shop a large sign over the door.

"I think you fellas can find it from here. Don't you?"

"Thanks, Red Beard, for your help."

They mounted and rode toward the sign Black Smith Shop. Quint and others around town had talked about the two missing strangers knowing they would be questioned. Quint was well aware of the sergeant coming to find out any information he could from him. He didn't know even how, Red Beard got here. Unless he told them. They wouldn't find out from him.

In the meantime, Frank, Jr found a rattle snake about eight feet long. He killed it and laid it by the trail leading into the forest hoping the soldiers would come that way to see if there were hoof prints in the ground near the woods. What a surprise! Those men could have fallen from their mounts if a rattler had struck at their horse. They could have scattered into the forest and been lost.

He was now dressed as a white man, hair pulled back as if cut, sport coat, dress trousers white shirt, tie and black shoes. He dressed especially for these men. They only had seen him in buckskins and moccasins. Now they had a surprise as his speech was much like the white man, although he wasn't about to forget his Injun upbringing.

His mother and sisters now spoke perfect English. The other tribe members and families had houses and became farmers, cattlemen, and some even worked in the small factory canning food products. What a difference from the people who the colonel at the fort called savages. He could use more education.

Frank, Jr's grandfather Winthrop was disgusted after he first met the colonel. He called his grandson a savage. Well, he let him know he didn't think much of him.

"Sir, you're referring to my grandson as a savage!"

Frank Jr. hadn't been questioned by them yet and they weren't sure just where to look for him. They went to the hotel after leaving the blacksmith shop. He asked Mrs. Winthrop might know something about his whereabouts. The two soldiers went to the Winthrop House, tied the horses to the hitching post, and went to the front door. Knocking twice.

Star came to the door, "Yes, Gentlemen, may I help you?"

They quickly removed their hats and ask politely, "Yes, are you Mrs. Winthrop?'

"I am Frank Winthrop's widow Star. What is it you wish?"

"Well, Ma'm, we wanted to talk with your son. I think he is known as Swift Eagle?"

"Yes, my son is at the local bank working. I think you will find him there."

"Thank you, Mrs. Winthrop." They returned to their horses looking around to find the bank sign down the street.

The local towns people came to their doors watching the soldiers go to the bank. Many of them walked behind to see what they wanted of Swift Eagle, they now knew him as Frank Jr. They left the horses at the hitching post and went inside.

Ms. Webster was at the teller's window. There was a neat lobby with table. They again removed their hat in presence of the lady teller.

"Good afternoon, Gentlemen, may I help you?"

"Yes, Miss, we are looking to speak with an Indian known as Swift Eagle. I think he is here."

"Yes, if you will wait just a moment I will see if he is busy."

They stood waiting, looking around the room. There was the American flag hanging in the corner. What a joke they thought an Indian running a bank like he was a real American.

They turned as they heard a door behind them open. To their surprise there stood a young man six feet tall, in sport coat, dress trousers, white shirt, tie, and black dress shoes, and haircut.

"Hello, I understand you are looking for me is there something I can do for you?"

They couldn't believe this was an educated man who spoke very correct English. They must have the wrong information.

"You see, Sir, we have been told a man by the name of Swift Eagle would be here. The lady told us he would be here."

"You've found him, what can I do for you?"

"There must be some mistake the man we're looking for is an Indian."

"I am a half-breed as my father, Frank Winthrop was white and married my mother, Morning Star."

"Yes, Sir, we met your mother, she directed us here."

"Would you like to come in my office and talk where it would be private?"

"Uh, no, Sir, we just wanted to ask if you knew of the two men who were looking for you some months ago."

"I heard a couple of men wanted to meet me, but I never met them. I was deer hunting when they left town. I guess you heard Colonel Custer, too, was looking for an Indian. I think and he found him. Chief Sitting Bull I believe."

"Uh, yes, thank you, Sir. Sorry to have troubled you."

"It's quite all right. Is there anything else?"

"No, you've answered our questions. We will report back to the fort as you say, you never met them."

They went outside. The people had gathered on the board-walk trying to listen what was being said inside. The soldiers mounted and rode out of town and on the road to the closed Dusty Road Trading Post. There they would take any papers and things pertinent to the United States Army. Then fill the canteen from the flowing well before going on to the fort.

33

The town was now growing, the church had been built, and David Brooks was still serving as the minister. Whitney and Sylvia were teaching Sunday school, learning the Ten Commandments and memorizing the twenty-third Psalm. Stories about the baby, Moses being left in a basket in the river, and King Solomon and the two women who claimed the same baby.

Whitney told them, "It tells the king was wise. He knew she was the real mother and gave her the baby."

The children enjoyed the stories. There was always Sunday dinner after Mr.Brooks hour of service. They enjoyed the dinner and fellowship with the people.

The town could use a dentist and a barber now. People were pleased with the growth of Black Water.

The Winthrop House still served as the hospital and offices of Dr. Jones and Dr. Young. Christmas time was coming Brad thought it would be nice if he and his nephew and family would visit Boston for the season. His niece, Sylvia and Strong Bow were married and expecting their first child. His mother would be anxious to come with them when they returned to see her next little great grandchild. He went to the bank to see if Frank Jr. was there. Miss Webster told him he was at Quint's. He went to the blacksmith's place. Sure enough the bank president was there in jeans poundings out a pair of horse shoes. Talking with Quint who was trimming the horse's hoof.

"Hey fellas take a break. I would like to talk with you a few minutes, Frank, if you have the time."

The men looked up and stopped a minute.

"Let me finish this, Uncle Brad, the horse is waiting for his shoe. Come have a seat on the bench."

They went on with their work while he watched, wondering how his nephew would rather do this than sit behind his desk at the bank. Finally, Frank came over while Quint nailed the horseshoe to the horse's hoof.

"What is it, Uncle Brad?" He wiped the sweat from his face on his shirt sleeve, went to the flowing well, and had a drink of water. He sat on the bench by Brad.

"Frank, I just was thinking since Christmas is coming soon it would be good if we were to take a trip to Boston and see my mother and father over Christmas. She might come back with us since Sylvia is expecting her papoose.

"Uh, that so Grandmother would like to see Little Eagle too. She not see him yet"

"Well, why don't you talk with Ruth. See if she would like to take a train ride to see her grandmother and grandfather. They would be happy to have us with them and I would like to go for Christmas."

"I will let you know, Uncle Brad." He got up, went to the anvil, and started shaping another horseshoe. Quint was trimming the other hoof, getting it ready.

Brad got up and went back to the hotel. He and Chief Lone Wolf had learned to play checkers. He was teaching the chief to play rummy. Brad was the foreman at the canning plant, keeping things running, and orders filled. The peach orchard was producing enough fruit now to can. The farms were storing hay for the winter and grain in the new silo. They built a large barn to store enough potatoes to supply the settlement during the winter months. They learned now to farm for their food and not have to hunt to survive. They would still hunt for their favorite venison and other wild animals. The smoke house was always full. A little education, money, and instructions had given them a different way of life.

Frank, Jr. talked with Ruth about going to visit grandparents over Christmas. She came to talk with Morning Star.

"Mother Star, Frank ask me about going to see grandparents at Christmas. I don't know if I want to go to Boston."

"I think it would be good for my son to see the place where his father was born."

"Yes, but I am afraid to leave Black Water."

"I understand, my daughter, why don't we talk with Dr. Young see if he can help you not be afraid."

She went with her daughter-in-law to his office. There was a patient waiting. After she patient left, Dr. Young ask Star and Ruth to come in. He sat behind his desk across from them.

"Dr. Young, my husband wants to go to Boston for Christmas. I am afraid to go. Can you help me not be afraid?"

"It's something unknown to you, nothing is wrong. I was afraid to come to Black Water."

"You were, Dr. Young, why?"

"The same reason you are afraid to go to Boston It's some-place different you don't know about. Most people are afraid when they are going to a strange place. I would say take the Christmas vacation and learn how people live in the big city, you will be surprised."

"Yes, Dr. Young, but I don't care how they live and I don't want to be surprised."

"I think you need to talk with your husband and perhaps he would go, take Little Eagle and Brad go without you, Ruth."

She never thought he would go without her. She didn't like it at all. She would go with them.

"You are right. I talk with Frank. Thank you Dr. Young."

They left the office and she went to see Frank at the bank. Little Eagle was with Little Faun in the living room playing on the floor with his toys.

34

Ruth had the luggage packed for her and Little Eagle, after her talk with Dr. Young, she wasn't about to let Frank and Little Eagle go and leave her here. Frank packed things he would wear. Every morning when he dressed his special knife was first in the sheath, strapped to his waist, under his shirt. He had made moccasins for the grandparents and Mary and Frank for their gifts.

They had never celebrated this in the camp only had celebrations when fall harvest is finished. They made big fire, danced with bells, songs, and drums. They had plenty venison and good fun. Some of the younger braves would wrestle. He thought about these things he remembered when he was a small boy before his father was killed.

They were ready to go. Brad met them at the hotel. He had his buggy waiting to take them to the train. Quint would ride with them to bring the rig back.

"Good bye, Mother Star," Ruth clung to her in tears. Little Eagle Wing was delighted, laughing, and anxiously waiting to go for a ride on the big train. They left from Winthrop House. Star and the others waved from the porch. Ruth dried her tears thinking she wouldn't be alone in Black Water over Christmas. They arrived at the station. The engine was there, the bell ringing, steam coming from it. Quint helped them take the luggage to the door. Standing there until the porter yelled, "All Aboard! All Aboard."

Ruth was shaking as she stepped up into the Pullman car. They went in to find their seats. The door was shut and the car started moving. She sat close to Frank Jr. shivering in fear.

Brad said, "Ruth look out the window. It's fun to see the different houses, farms, and land as we travel along."

She peeked out the window, there was a little filly with its mother running, kicking, and bucking in the pasture. It brought a smile to her face. The day went by swiftly and the porter came through.

"Dinner is served in the dining car." She looked over at Brad wondering what now?

"Come on let's go see what they have to eat in there."

They followed him to the car. He found a table. The porter came to take the order.

They were serving baked turkey, dressing, gravy, cranberry sauce, and coffee, tea, milk or orange juice. Brad ordered for the three of them and ask Little Eagle if he wanted juice or milk. After dinner, Brad thought it would be much more comfortable in the observation car. They decided to go there. It was better for Ruth. She now was getting accustomed to the clickety, clack of the wheels on the rails, and begin to relax smiling once in a while. They left returning to the sleeper car. They would reach Boston tonight.

35

The whistle blowing, bell ringing, and the porter shouting, "Boston, Boston coming into Boston."

The passengers gathered their luggage, the porter helped them down the steps, and placed their luggage on the side walk near them. Brad looked around for his father's carriage. He saw them, waved, and shouted, "Hey, Ben, over here, Father here we are. Come on Frank let's go meet them."

He and Frank took the luggage, Ruth held Little Eagle who was waving, and shouting, "Grandfather, grandfather."

Ben and Mr. Winthrop came quickly help with the luggage.

Frank, Jr. looked over at him surprised. He thought he must have heard him talking with another Indian who hadn't learned English. He knew his grandfather didn't care and loved his grandchildren. They were hugged and hurried to the carriage. It was starting to snow and the dusk was closing in. Little Eagle was delighted seeing the Christmas lights on the street as they traveled to Grandfather's house. Old Dobbin sure knew the way home.

"Ben, how have you and Martha been since I've been gone? I missed you."

"Yas, sir, Mr. Brad we is been jus' fine and yo parents is jus' fine, too."

Frank Jr wondered what tribe this black man came from. He had never heard them talk before. He would ask Uncle Brad. He remembered reading in school and seeing pictures of the black people. They were called slaves. He wouldn't like the way the slaves were treated. He was glad Ben was here in Boston with Grandfather. Ben pulled up in front of a large house at the edge of town. The light was on and Grandmother came out to the carriage. She took Little Eagle in her arms.

"Grandmother, Grandmother me glad to see you."

Frank Jr. thought his son's speech again strange.

She kissed his cheek and said, "Me glad to see you too little Winthrop boy."

He laughed and hugged his grandmother. They went up the steps and inside. It was cozy and warm Ruth thought. She looked at the lovely furniture and rug on the floor. The room was a delight. She found a chair in the corner and went to it. Martha came in with hot chocolate and marshmallows.

"Welcome home Mr. Brad, Missus Ruth and Mr. Frank Jr. We is glad you is here with us. Ain't we, Miss Mary?"

"Yes, Martha. Isn't my little grandson adorable?"

"He sho is and likes the chocolate, too."

He had it all over him and licking the marshmallow off the spoon. Everyone was laughing at him.

"Grandmother Mary, I will wash him if you show me our room," Ruth said.

Martha answered, "Come here chile. I'll sho you de room upstairs."

"Frank, will you bring my luggage upstairs?" She followed Martha and took Little Eagle Winn to the bathroom, washed the chocolate off, and put his panamas on. They went back to the living room.

"Look at you now, nice, clean, and ready for bed now little Winthrop?" Mary said. She had found some of the toys her boys had from years ago and gave them to him to play with. There was a toy soldier, a fire truck, and a little wagon. He was having fun with them. She sat with tears thinking of his grandfather, who would never have the opportunity to see his grandson.

"Well now let's not think about it, Miss Mary." Martha said.

"Brad, I think if it continues to snow, we can get the sleigh out. You know it's up to you to buy the tree, so we can all enjoy seeing it decorated."

"Mother, tomorrow we will get the tree. If it snows enough, we will go sleigh riding tomorrow."

Frank Winthrop sat puffing his pipe, watching his great grandson, and was happy to have them here for the holidays. They were called to dinner. Martha prepared roast beef, mashed potatoes, gravy, and English peas. They sat with bowed head as Frank Sr. blessed the food and thanked the Almighty for their safe trip. Little Eagle Winn thoroughly enjoyed the mashed potatoes and ate the peas with his fingers. Grandmother Mary enjoyed watching and laughing at him. He was unconcerned about it. The spoon was too much trouble. When they finished eating, Frank, Jr. lifted him out of his highchair.

"Tell Grandmother good night, Son". Frank Jr. He ran to his grandmother and hugged her she kissed his cheek, his dad took him upstairs to their room. Ruth had placed pillows and heavy comforter on the floor by their bed. She laid him on them, covered him, kissed him saying, "Night, little Winthrop boy. I love you."

He smiled at her, snuggled up, and soon was fast asleep. She lay on the bed weary from the two days on the train.

Frank called to her, "Are you coming back Ruth?"

"No, I think I will go to bed now Frank. Say good night grandmother."

"Good night dear, I will be up soon."

Frank Jr. sat and visited with the family for some time then came to bed. He gently kissed his young son and eased in beside Ruth to keep from waking her. They slept soundly for the remainder of the night.

The snow was gently falling and if it remained on the ground, they would take the sleigh and go for a ride tomorrow, Brad told him.

The smell of coffee brewing woke Frank Jr. He quietly slipped out of bed, left the two sleeping, dressed, and hurried downstairs to have breakfast with Brad and his grandparents. Before long, Ruth and little Winn joined them. Martha served pancakes sausage, scrambled eggs, hot chocolate, and hot coffee. It was delicious.

"Frank Jr. let's go and get the sleigh from the shed, cleaned up, and get ready to go for a ride. Old Dobbin will enjoy pulling it and hearing the sleigh bells."

They went out to work on getting the sleigh ready. Mary Elizabeth had her own agenda planned. She would let her Ladies Club members know her Indian grandson, his wife, and child were here for the Christmas season. She planned to have welcome dinner for them at the Red

Dragon Restaurant. She wanted to show the aristocrats of Boston the Winthrop's were not prejudiced.

Her help had been with them since her boys were young they had been given their freedom papers and left the South. Their daughter, Patricia, was in England living with Randy Swain's parents, Lord and Lady Swain while attending college.

Ben and Martha, felt fortunate to have been hired by the Winthrop's and have a home with them. When Randy Swain found about their daughter wanting to go to college, he immediately contacted his parents and they graciously invited her to come live with them and attend school in England. Ben and Martha were so grateful to know they would take good care of their daughter. They had been able to save from their salary the Winthrop's paid them and now sent Patricia an allowance each month. She also worked in the book store on weekends. She met many fine people and it helped her finances.

Mary was making a list of those in the Lady's Club so she could send invitations. She needed R.S.V.P.'s to be sure the Red Dragon could prepare for everyone.

Bradley Sr. said, "Mary dear, would you like me to go with you to make a reservation at the Red Dragon? We should reserve the complete dining room and invite your club members as a welcome party for our grandchildren."

"Yes dear I want the Cheng's, May Lyn and Lee, to understand our grandson is an American Indian and our other guests are African. They also must have seen prejudice as they are Chinese."

"I agree, Dear, we will have Ben and Brad get the carriage ready and go make the reservation this afternoon."

36

Ben came around to the front with the carriage in the afternoon. Brad would accompany his mother and father to make the reservation at the Red Dragon for their welcome dinner. She would also send invitations to each club member.

"Thank you for getting the carriage." Mary said. Frank, Sr. came out and climbed in with them. Ben clicked to old Dobbin and off they went trotting along the street. The snow was blowing and Mary Elizabeth pulled her scarf close around her face.

"This is good Christmas weather Mother," Brad told her.

"Yes, Son, I remember you and Frank with your sleds and the Christmas tree with your toys under it on Christmas morning."

"Now Mother you have more children to enjoy around the Christmas tree." He hugged his mother, seeing tears in her eyes.

Frank, Sr. just sat quiet, with memories of his son who was killed, by a thief he caught stealing his fur pelts. He thought

Frank would rather hunt for food and furs to sell than live here in comfort with his family. They knew it was what their son had wanted. He had written telling them how happy he was and he married a beautiful young Indian maiden. The chief had conducted the marriage ceremony and he had been made a blood brother. Then after a couple of years he had written about the two children she had born for him. He planned to bring them to visit. He never had the chance.

About this time, Ben pulled in at the Red Dragon Restaurant, He got out, and tied Dobbin to the hitching post in front. Then he came and assisted Frank, Sr. down and Mrs. Winthrop. They went to the front door. Ben quickly opened the door for them. He went back to the carriage.

They stood a moment inside, the Cheng's came to them, bowed and said, "Ah, good day Missy and Mr. Winthrop we are honored with your visit. How may we serve you?"

"Mr. Cheng, my wife and I would like to engage your restaurant for a party to welcome our grandson and his family for a Christmas visit. I wasn't sure if we could engage the complete restaurant."

Lee looked at May Lyn, in wonder. They were stunned for a moment then, Chen Lee answered, "Why, yes, of course, Mr. Winthrop. We would need to let other customers know the time we would be closed for your party."

"Mrs. Winthrop plans to invite the woman's club and their husbands. We want to introduce our grandson, his wife, and child as they are visiting. We will also have our house keeper and her husband. You see it is why we wanted to ask you first. I know you may have encountered prejudice. We wish our friends to know these people are our family members.

"Yes, we understand, let us know in advance the time you wish the party. We will be honored to serve your friends and your family. Please let us know how many will be coming. Then I will tell you the cost."

"Very good, Mr. Cheng, thanks to you both we will be in touch." The Cheng's bowed as they left.

There were dinner guest's listening, who overheard their conversation, whispering to each other. They heard their son married an Indian out west somewhere. The son had children with the Indian woman. Also, they knew the Winthrop's were of the upper class and held mortgages in town.

The next day Mary Elizabeth sent invitations to all of the club members. She also included the fact her Indian grandson and his family were the ones being honored with the dinner party.

After they returned, Brad bought the Christmas tree, fresh oranges and apples from the corner store. They had a fun time decorating it. Martha made popcorn and Mary Elizabeth showed Ruth how to string it. Little Winn was held up so he could place the star on the top. He was clapping and laughing as his grandfather lit the candles on the tree. He had never seen this before. They enjoyed his laughter and joy as much as the little boy.

• • • • •

Brad, Ben, and Frank Jr. had the sleigh ready. They hitched Old Dobbin to it and pulled around to the front door. Everyone bundled up and went for a sleigh ride. Mary Elizabeth, and Frank, Sr. laughing along with the others. It had been years since they had gone sleigh riding. The roads were iced over, there were snow flurries which made it more like Christmas.

"Uncle Brad, you told me your creek was so wide I couldn't see the trees on the other side, and you were going to show me," Little Winn told him.

Brad turned Old Dobbin around and headed for the bay. A freight boat was just coming in the harbor. The fog horn blew.

"Father, is it a bear?" Little Winn ask.

"No, it's not a bear Little Eagle, I don't know what it is."

Brad laughed. "Frank, it's a fog horn. It sounds, at intervals to keep the ships from wrecking and knowing there are ships in the harbor and ocean close by so they don't crash."

"How do they make it sound at one time? Then quiet and then sound again, Uncle Brad?"

"The waves or swells cause the buoy to lean one way and then the other way causing the wind to blow through the horn on the buoy."

"And now what is a buoy?'

"It is a large like cork on a string which is tied to the bottom of the ocean you know like a cork on a fishing string?"

"Now I understand and Randy will be glad to hear about this when we return home. It makes good sense, Uncle Brad. We didn't read about it at school."

"I guess Randy never thought of talking about it. There are many things to teach everyone."

They turned back toward the house.

"Tomorrow, Little Eagle, I will show you the creek in the day time. You will be able to see it better. I will show you a skating pond you will like, too."

"What's a skating pond, Uncle Brad?" he asked.

"You wear shoes with blades on the bottom like the sleigh has and you slide really fast over the ice."

Ruth and Frank Jr. were listening, too, wondering about the skating. They heard about but hadn't seen it yet.

Brad drove Dobbin on to the house, let Ruth, Little Eagle, and his parents out in front. He and Frank Jr. went to the shed to unhitch Dobbin and the sleigh. After settling Dobbin and giving him a block of hay, they closed the shed and went in for the night. Martha had hot coffee and hot chocolate. Little Winn was already in bed. The others soon retired for the night. It had been a very pleasant holiday sleigh ride and evening.

• • • • •

The next day Mary Elizabeth told Brad she wished to go shopping for Christmas gifts. She asked him drive her to the stores. She asked Ruth if she would like to come and buy some things to take back to her friends in Black Water. She thought it would be nice to buy something for them to have on Christmas morning. Of course, Brad would take care of all the family.

Frank and his grandfather agreed to keep Winn while the ladies shopped. First, his Uncle Brad drove him to see the harbor with the boats and horn. The creek really was so big Little Eagle couldn't see any trees across the other side. They laughed at him. They went on to the skating pond. He wanted to skate, too. Brad rented a pair of skates with double runners. They had a fun time until it was time to take his mother shopping. They went back to the house. Lunch was ready when they got there. After eating a sandwich and bowl of chicken soup, Frank and Little Eagle went up to their room and took a nap. Mary, Ruth, and Brad went shopping.

Mary Elizabeth met several of her club friends and introduced them to her granddaughter Ruth. They were surprised when they met the lovely young woman. She was certainly different from what they expected. They told Mary Elizabeth they were looking forward to the party.

When they came home Little Eagle was playing with the toys in the living room. Martha had baked ham with pineapple slices, brown sugar, and cherries. It was different from what they had in the west. They enjoyed the ham with sweet potatoes, dressing, gravy, biscuits, butter, and peach jam. The little Winn was covered with jam enjoying every bite, of his biscuit. Everyone enjoyed watching him more than eating. After eating his mother took him, cleaned him up, and put him down for a short nap. The ladies retired to the kitchen to wrap gifts, Martha helped them they sipped egg nog and talked while the men sat in the living room. Of course, the fellows had egg nog also. After the ladies had retired for the night and the men were still in the living room talking.

Ben came in and said, "Mr. Bradley, they's somebody prowlin' in de shed out back. Dobbins stompin'..."

Before he finished talking, Frank, Jr. was out the front door, around the back there was a man had Dobbin bridled and was on his back, trying to get out the shed door. Frank, Jr. quickly drew his knife and threw it so the handle hit the culprits head, causing Dobbin to rear up. The thief's head struck against the timbers of the roof, he lost his balance, and fell to the ground still clutching the reins in his hand. Frank, Jr. heard a cracking sound as the man's head hit the ground. It sounded like his neck broke. By then Brad and Ben were there. Frank, Jr went and felt to see if the man was alive. He gathered his knife quickly and slid it in the sheath under his shirt.

"I think this man is dead, Uncle Brad."

"What happened to him, Frank?"

"I grabbed the reins, the horse reared up, he struck his head on the roof, he lost his balance, and he fell. I heard a crack like his neck broke."

Ben stood there his eyes wide open, "Lordy, Lordy what ya know, Mista Brad?"

Brad went over and felt to see if the man was still alive. He was dead. The horse was standing snorting, but not stepping on the thief.

"We must go get the police at once." The three hurried back to the living room.

"Father, a man was trying to steal Dobbin. He fell, broke his neck, and is dead. W must send for the police."

"Son, there is a station just two blocks up the street you and Frank go let them know." They put on heavy coats and started to the police station.

Ben went back to his room and Frank, Sr. waited for them to return.

The police came with them. They showed them the man lying there with the reins still clutched in his hand.

The Sergeant said, "Officer Riley, run back to the station and bring the wagon."

"Yes, sir, Sergeant." He was back in no time with the wagon to cart the body to the mortuary. The two lifted the corpse onto the wagon covered it with canvas. The sergeant said, "Mr. Winthrop, I will come back in the morning to get a full report on the incident." They drove on off. Brad and Frank went inside.

"Frank, you didn't knock him down? I know but you were right over him when we got there. I am not doubting you, bit it looked as if you picked up something."

"Uncle Brad, I did. I picked up the man's hand to see if he was dead or not."

"I know when I went over to him he had two knots on his head one on top and the other on the side of his head."

"I wonder how that happened. I saw him when he hit the timber although he could have hit another timber on the fall from the horse. Do you think I hit him Uncle Brad? Believe me, I would have to keep him from stealing the horse. Yes, I guess it could be, but you know the police will question all of us."

"Uncle Brad, I didn't kill the man if you are thinking I did. I heard his neck crack when he hit the ground. I wouldn't stop if someone were trying to hurt one of my people."

"I understand my only thought is the questioning by the police."

"Stop, Uncle Brad, I told you. I didn't kill the thief!"

Brad knew his nephew wouldn't hesitate to kill if his family was endangered. This wasn't the case and he believed him. Brad hated the questions from the police.

They went to the living room Brad explained to his dad and they had a shot of bourbon before retiring for the night.

Grandfather said, "It's for medicinal purposes to calm the nerves." Frank, Jr. looked at him not believing what he said.

Brad winked at his nephew.

He bid them good night and went up to bed and quietly lay beside his wife not to awaken her. The house settled into quietness and slumber.

•••••

After breakfast Mary Elizabeth asked Brad if he would hitch up Dobbin and take her to the Red Dragon. She wished to make the reservation for the twentieth. They would closed for the evening. She had already sent the invitations. She wanted to know how much food the Cheng's would need to prepare for them.

37

In the afternoon they had a visit from the police. By now the ladies had heard about the man trying to steal the horse. Everyone was waiting in the living room to see what the police sergeant had to say.

Brad answered the door, "Come in gentlemen and have a seat."

The sergeant and his officer removed their hats and found seats near the door.

Brad introduced them to the others. The sergeant looked over at Brad's father and said, "Mr. Winthrop would you kind of give me a run down on just what happened last night? How did you find out the man was in the barn?"

Frank Winthrop, Sr, cleared his throat and answered, "Well, Sir, we were preparing to go to bed when Ben, my diver, came in saying he heard noises coming from the shed where the horse was. Ben and his wife have rooms at the back of house. Immediately my grandson ran out back and found a man on the horse. He had the bridle on him and was trying to get him to go out to the barn. My grandson, Frank, Jr. can explain what happened next."

They looked over at Frank, Jr, who said, "When I saw he had the reins I reached for them. It frightened the horse who reared up. The man struck his head against the ceiling timbers, lost his balance and fell to the ground still grasping the reins. I heard a sharp crack as his head hit the ground, then ran over to see if he was still breathing. He wasn't. By then my uncle and Ben were there. My uncle checked to see if the man was alive."

He looked over at Brad. "I felt to see if he had a heartbeat. I didn't find one, which is when we ran to your station to let you know what had happened. Have you found out who he was?

"From what we have found so far, he came in on the freighter the other night and apparently had a fight and was in the brig until they came in port. I think he was from England, the captain is looking into his back ground now. We have all we need for now, Gentlemen, but there may be an inquest. You will most likely need to tell what you just told me."

The men stood up. Brad and his father went to the door with them, shook hands and they left.

"I hope we don't have to attend the inquest as we were planning to catch the train on the twenty-eighth to go home," Frank, Jr. said.

"Son, if you have to be here, there's nothing we can do about it. Until the matter is settled to their satisfaction and the case closed." Grandfather told Frank Jr.

He knew his grandfather was right so he would just relax. He knew his mother and Sheriff Buck Henry would take care of the bank while they were gone. Brad was into the banking business, too. Miss Webster and Brad had dated a couple times but nothing serious had come of it.

Mary Elizabeth was planning to return to Black Water with her son and grandchildren. She hoped to be there when her granddaughter, Sylvia, gave birth to her baby. She purchased all kinds of baby things to bring to them.

38

The dinner party was tonight. Mary Elizabeth was excited and ready to show off her grandchildren to the elite of Boston. She knew they had whispered about her Indian grandchildren behind her back and black people living in their home. It was time she set them straight. She knew she and her husband could buy and sell these people who called themselves aristocratic, upper class. It took more than what they had. It took good breeding. Indians and black folks knew what honor, courtesy, and consideration for others was. At least after tonight, they would know where she stood, especially the Woman's Club.

They were already. Everyone looked handsome, the men in their dinner jackets, white shirts and black ties. The ladies had long evening gowns and patent slippers, Ruth wore a lovely beaded band around her long black hair, which she left down. Martha had a little band of flowers across her head and Mary Elizabeth had a band of Indian beads like her granddaughter's.

They climbed into the carriage and off they went to the party. Just for the fun of it, Brad attached the sleigh bells to Dobbins harness. It was a festive occasion. The other carriages were arriving. They were parked all around the restaurant. The most stores had a hitching posts on either side of the street.

The Chengs greeted everyone at the door. The smell of food was sensational. A lovely buffet set up along one wall. Guests would be able to help themselves.

Soft oriental music played and Chinese lanterns were lit along the walls. After everyone was seated Frank Winthrop, Sr. stood. He tapped the knife on the water glass.

"May I have your attention, Friends. We invited you tonight to meet our grandchildren. This is their first trip to Boston. As many of you recall our son Frank being adventurous, went west to see how it was in the wilderness. He fell in love with an Indian. They were married by Chief Lone Wolf. After Frank's death we wanted his children to meet our friends. Please stand, Frank Jr.

He stood up wondering what next. His wife Ruth. Please stand. Mary is holding our great grandson, Winn. Hold him up so he can say hello to our friends. She stood up with little Winn kissing his cheek. He was laughing gleefully. The group stood and applauded.

The president of the Ladies Club said, "We would be honored to have your grandson Frank Jr. speak for us about the ways of his people at our club meeting before they leave, if he would be so kind."

Everyone sat back down. Frank, Jr continued standing. Brad wondered what he had in mind.

His nephew surprised him when he said, "Missus, I thank you for the invitation to speak at your club meeting. I would be most honored to speak for you."

This brought another round of applause.

Grandfather then stood. "Now friends let us enjoy some of the Cheng's delicious food they have prepared for us. You may serve yourselves at the buffet. The guests lined up at the buffet. The food was a delight, sweet and sour chicken, pork ribs, fried rice, chow mein, spicy jasmine tea, steaks, pork chops, or seafood. They had a wonderful evening and the Winthrop's stood at the door as the guest left. The men shaking hands and the ladies thanking each other graciously. Martha and Ben were quiet and definitely enjoyed being included as family with the Winthrop's.

Needless to say Brad was wondering what his Indian nephew would speak about at the Ladies' Club. His father was surprised at his speaking. He thought him, too, shy. They both had much to learn about this man.

One of the stock holders in Frank Winthrop's Ship Yard stopped as they were leaving saying, "Frank, would you ask your grandson if he would be guest speaker at our business meeting next Monday?"

"Yes, of course, JB. I will if they are in town I am sure he would be glad to."

Brad ran out and drove the carriage around to the front of the restaurant. The ladies came out and Brad helped them into the carriage. Frank, Sr. waited until the last guest left. He shook hands with Cheng Lee and said, "Thank you. It was a perfect evening and dinner. We are most pleased."

The Chengs bowed. "You most welcome, honorable Winthrop. Good evening."

He then joined, Brad, Frank, Jr., and Ben climbing into the front seat. Brad drove them on to the house, pulling up at the front door. He ran up the steps to unlock the door. Frank and

Ben helped the others down. Soon they were in the house and said good night.

Brad and Frank, Jr. lingered a while in the living room talking. Brad served them another small brandy. Brad looked at Frank, Jr handing him a glass saying, "Ahem, just for medicinal purposes, you know."

They laughed knowing it was a phrase often used by Frank, Sr. Brad had seen his dad take a snort at the club.

"What topic are you going to speak about at the Ladies' Club, Frank?"

"I don't exactly know. I might tell them how we survived the animals, storms lightening, and harsh winters."

"Those would be a good topics. I think they would enjoy it."

"We will do something. Perhaps you could give me some ideas, Uncle Brad."

"Right now I am ready for some shut eye. I will see you at breakfast unless some other dandy tries to steal our horse." He laughed and going up to his room.

Frank. Jr. followed to settle in for the night. He lay thinking about what he would say at their meeting. How the Indians were rounded up like cattle and shipped to barren land, little game, no food, and left to starve? They wouldn't want to hear about who the real savages are.

He recalled as a small boy hearing the elders talking around the fire about the Thunder Bird Spirit God who brought them to the earth. It was said, the Thunder Bird Spirit God flew through the sky, a white tail of smoke behind it. The story went on to say some of those on their earth wanted to inspect on this wilderness and were left there to establish a tribe and live. He knew one thing. They apparently survived. The others thought they didn't survive living on their land after the white man came. They set up corners and pushed the Indians farther from their lands.

After he learned to read and had an education he could understand how the white man robbed them of their land and way of life. He would try to tell the story of their camp, the celebration of the harvest, and the rituals handed down to them. He soon drifted to sleep, dreaming of his wedding ceremony with his wife, Ruth.

•••••

The next morning at breakfast, Frank Jr. told Brad he would speak at the ladies meeting and ask if he would introduce him. He wanted attend the meeting with him.

"Do you think we will have time before we leave for Black Water?"

"Yes, Uncle Brad. I will tell them of the way we hunt and how we enjoyed our wedding ceremony things we passed down. I will not tell how I found the man that killed my father."

"Well, Frank, you never told me how you found the man."

"No, Uncle Brad? I just found him. It is all you need to know, except he will never do kill again."

Brad shivered when he saw the look in his nephew's eyes.

•••••

Brad and his mother contacted the president of the Ladies' Club. The date was set and Brad was there with his nephew to make the introduction.

"Good evening, Ladies. I am pleased to introduce my nephew Frank Winthrop, Jr. He will speak on the lives of Indians. Brad sat back down.

Frank, Jr. stood up to a round of applause. He then began "First, let me thank you for inviting me to speak at your meeting. I will begin where I was born at the Dust Road Trading Post reservation camp. Mother was delighted to present my father, Frank Winthrop with a healthy squalling son. My father gave the Indian war shout at birth. My father, Tall Brave Man Frank, was proud of his son.

I was taught early to use my bow and arrow if I wanted food. I learned to traverse the brush silently and use the arrow accurately as I hunted for rabbits or squirrel. The big game came later when I could handle my knife.

My mother, Morning Star, would cook game over the hot coals of the fire we kept burning all night. I would learn to wash off in the creek which ran by the camp. I learned early to sleep on the ground with a blanket to cover the leaves and moss. My mother knew how to work and tan the animal hides to make our clothing. She made corn pone a sort of bread and baked it in the coals of the camp fire."

He dressed in his buckskins, a beaded strip of buckskin around his head, and left his hair down. They were certainly impressed with Mary Winthrop's' grandson. One of the lady's young daughter was smitten with this young man. He couldn't help but notice her forwardness. He was sure his uncle Brad was aware of it, too. Frank, Jr. told of the wedding ceremony and the food the tribeswomen prepared. Later how they danced with the sounds of bells, drums, and chanting.

"You see, Ladies, our only means of survival was the wild animals we hunted in the forest. When the white man shoved the Indian off of our land we had no game and the land wasn't good for raising corn or any food. I am sure you know from the history books, many of my people died of starvation. We are still surviving though and things are getting better."

"I now have a bank. We have a new town. I was allowed to attend school and get an education. My son now will have an education. I have to thank my grandfather, Frank Winthrop for the advantages I now enjoy. If you have questions, I will be glad to answer them now."

Brad thought uh oh, when the young daughter rushed to talk to Frank, Jr. Brad wasn't surprised when his nephew politely ignored her advances toward him. Frank, Jr. told the club members he would send moccasins from Black Water for the club members. Soon after being served cake and coffee he and Brad took their leave.

Placing his coffee cup on the table, he stood and saying, "Thank you, Ladies, for inviting me. I hope you will visit us in Black Water someday."

He and Brad made their way to the door amidst applause and were happy to get outside. It was a good thing Ruth didn't see the girl swooning over her husband. Frank had been amused and politely ignoring her.

39

The next day Brad decided to drive Frank and Little Winn to the Boston Sea Port where he could see the ships and freighters. He had forgotten the freighters were coming in later in the night. All of a sudden, he remembered the police sergeant said the man caught trying to steal their horse was a sailor from a freighter. He had been in the brig the sergeant told them, after being in a fight. They guessed it accounted for the abrasions on his face and head other than where he hit the cross beam in the barn when the horse reared up. He hoped it would be the end of it. He didn't say anything to Frank. They stopped at the dock. Brad asked, "Little Winn, would you like to walk on the dock and see how big the ship is? Then we can go to the creek too."

Little Winn was excited. Frank was also interested in seeing the freighter up close. It was the SS Goldstar. Brad tied Dobbin to the hitching post and they walked on to the end of the dock where the freighter was docked. The deck hands were swabbing the deck and looked up as they approached. Seeing the little boy, they stopped and waved to him. Frank was over whelmed at the height of the hull of the freighter.

"The hull on this boat is very high, Uncle Brad." He was looking up it seemed the hull leaned over them as it was near the top and deck. There was a red line along the hull from the bow to the stern of the freight boat. What is that line for, Uncle Brad?"

"It is called the water line. When the boat is loaded the boat sinks in the water to the line. You see now it has been unloaded the boat has risen up above the water line."

"I wouldn't like it. I would rather hunt for food to eat than work for the boat people."

"It's one way of putting it, Frank. I am with you though, I wouldn't want to be a sailor. Dad can build the ships at his ship yard, but someone else can sail them for my part."

"I will talk with Randy Swain when I get home. He would like to know about the freighter, too."

Frank lifted Little Winn to his shoulders and they walked back to the carriage.

"Let's go have something to eat at the skating pond, Frank. I want to let Little Winn see the people skating."

They drove on back to the park where some boys were on the pond having fun racing after each other.

"Uncle Brad, me want to skate now."

Frank looked at his son again wondering why he was talking this way since he had learned to speak correctly. He then remembered, Chief Lone Wolf had been talking to the boy. He didn't say anything. Hoping it would pass he when he started school. They went to a food vendor in the park.

"What do you want to eat, Frank?"

Little Winn said. "Me want food, too, Uncle Brad."

Frank then said loudly, I want hot food, too, Uncle Brad."
He looked sternly at his son. Brad caught it but didn't say anything. He went to the window and ordered

"We would like three hot sandwiches and three chocolate milk." They stood at the counter until the sandwiches were ready. They sat on the bench eating and watching the boys on the pond. Little Winn sat kicking his heels under the bench enjoying the food and the park. Frank thought this was different than eating at the Winthrop Hotel dining room. They didn't have food stands like this. It was like eating around the camp fire, rabbits, squirrel, and venison but with a hot biscuit.. This was good.

Brad asked where they could rent a pair of double runner skated. The food vendor handed him a pair. They laughed as Little Winn tried to skate like the boys did. He soon realized he couldn't skate.

Ruth took Little Winn, washed his face and hands, then between his jabbering about skating, she settled him down for a nap. The men had a snooze in the living room. Frank, Sr. and Mary Elizabeth came in quietly. They had been out with friends for lunch. There were just two more days until Christmas, Frank, Jr. hoped they could start home right after. He was ready to get home to Black Water. They awakened when the elder Winthrops came in the living room.

"Hey, Father, I didn't hear you and mother come in. How was your lunch?"

"As usual, Son, however I did see the police sergeant who told me they had found out about the man who tried to steal Dobbin. He was wanted in England for burglary. There won't be any inquest so when you wish to go to Black Water you may."

Frank thought thank goodness. He had enough of the big city. When they were alone later Frank told Brad they should go to the train station and buy their tickets so they could be ready to board the train without waiting in line.

Brad said, "We can go first thing in the morning. I will be glad to get back home, too."

Frank thought it was strange coming from his uncle. Since he had been raised here in Boston.

Christmas Eve, everyone placed gifts under the tree. Little Winn wanted to open them. His father was stern with him. "No, Little Winn, in the morning you can open them. You will have lots to open, but not tonight."

"Me want me toy now, Daddy."

"What did you say young man?"

"Me want me toy now."

"No, say I want my toy?"

"You want your toy Daddy?" Everyone laughed

"Good going, Frank. I think you get the point don't you?"

The grandparents said it was no use trying to and explain about the red suited guy called Santa Claus to this little boy.

They had chocolate cake and Little Winn was covered with chocolate. His mother cleaned him up, put his sleeper on, and lay down with him until he fell asleep. She came back down stairs and enjoyed some cake and coffee before retiring for the night. It was a happy Christmas Eve. Grandfather and grandmother were grateful for their grandchildren and sat smiling thinking of their blessings.

The next morning the little boy was first to see his toys under the Christmas tree. He had never seen a three wheel tricycle. It was the only toy her had an interest in, although he opened many packages. Mary Elizabeth thought we can pack these and take them with us on the train. He was all over the living room, kitchen, and having the time of his life on his trike. He put his toy soldier on the back and rode it all around.

Ruth was delighted with a pair of silk pajamas, robe, and slippers to match and loved a bottle of perfume.

Mary Elizabeth had a lovely diamond watch and ring.

Frank, Sr. had a brand new pipe and pouch for his tobacco plus a can of Old Granger cut tobacco.

Brad has two new shirts a pair of socks. Frank, Jr. had socks two western shirts He and Brad each had new wrist watches. There were gifts for Martha and Ben. They enjoyed a breakfast of hot biscuits, scrambled eggs, sausage, and coffee. After they sat talking in the living room while Martha straightened up the kitchen. Ruth went to help but Martha wouldn't hear of it.

Brad said, "Mother, we are going to buy the tickets to Black Water tomorrow. I wondered if you still planned to go with us."

Mary Elizabeth sat silent a moment then looked at her husband. "Dear, would you mind if I were to go for say a month or so? I would love to see our new grandchild."

"Harump, uh." He coughed and cleared his throat.

"Of course not, Dear. I think I can manage for a month, but don't stay any longer." They laughed at him.

Brad then said, "What if I get old Dobbin hitched to the sleigh this afternoon and we all take a Christmas Day ride around town. I will be sure Dobbin is decked out with tinsel, sleigh bells, and red ribbons?"

"Say what a great idea, Uncle Brad. I think it would be a memory before we take the train back to Black Water."

"I would enjoy it too, Dear." Mary Elizabeth told her son.

Little Winn was always ready to go for a ride in the carriage or sleigh and Ruth enjoyed it, but more reserved and quiet. After they had a delicious dinner of baked turkey, dressing, gravy, cranberry sauce, sweet potatoes, and sweet green peas, Brad hitched old Dobbin to the sleigh and pulled around to the front porch.

"All right, Everybody. Come on, let's go for an old fashioned Christmas sleigh ride."

Brad helped his mother down the steps and into the sleigh. Ruth came with Little Winn, then Frank, Sr. climbed in front beside Frank Jr. finally, Brad got in, grabbed the reins, and looked back at the ladies in back.

"Are you ready for an old fashioned Christmas sleigh ride over the river and through the woods?"

"Ready, over the river and through the woods to grandmother's house we go," Mary Elizabeth sang.

"Get up, Dobbin. Let's go." The horse started trot sleigh bells ringing,

"Jingle Bells, jingle all the way," Their neighbors came out on the porches waving and shouting, "Merry Christmas, Winthrops."

They continued singing carols while they road through the neighborhood, waving to neighbors, who mistook them for carolers.

Little Winn was jumping, laughing, and shouting, "Merry Christmas!" He was enjoying himself, and he brought love and laughter to the hearts of the adults.

40

The next morning after breakfast Brad said, "Frank, what do you say we go buy the train tickets? The next train will be leaving in two more days, bound for Tennessee."

The men walked to the train depot and purchased the tickets.

When they were ready to leave, they took to take a cab to the depot. His mother was already packed and had an extra suitcase with baby things for the new great grandchild. They had boxed Little Winn's tricycle and toys and shipped those two days before so he could enjoy them at home. Frank thought the two days would never go by. He was ready to go home. Brad helped his mother up the steps to the train, Frank, Jr. and Ruth were next with Little Winn. They found their seats and sat waiting.

The train started to move. They settled down and leaned back. Ruth drew a sigh of relief thinking, she was glad to be going home to her own little house. They watched the trees and buildings slip behind them as the train move slowly at first then gathered speed. Mary Elizabeth had the color book, crayons, and a children's story book to read to Little Winn, to keep her great grandson occupied on the two day trip home. This little boy was as full of life as was his grandfather, Frank had been at his age. She sat thinking of her son Frank and his offspring. How grateful she was to have them.

After an hour or so the little boy fell asleep in his grandmother's lap. Frank, Jr. picked him up and they went to the observation car. There was more room and comfort with the little boy sleeping

After supper they retired to their bunks. Little Winn slept in the bunk with his mother. Everyone was lulled to sleep with the clacking of the wheels on the rails. They awakened to the porter walking through the sleeper car announcing breakfast.

"Breakfast is served in the dining car. Breakfast is served in the dining car."

They quickly dressed, brushed teeth, hair, washed up, then joined each other for breakfast.

Little Eagle was ready for breakfast. "Me hungry, Mother, me hungry."

"Come on, Little Winn," his mother said.

Frank and the others joined them in the hall. They found a place in the dining car and waited for the menu. The porter took the orders enjoyed fresh orange juice, scrambled eggs, hash browns, toast, jelly, and coffee. They finished and returned to the observation car. They would arrive home the next afternoon. Ruth held her son, singing to him until he fell asleep after lunch. Mary Elizabeth leaned in her chair, closed her eyes, and rested. Frank sat beside his wife and son.

Brad found a chair near the window where he could see. He was reading about the Wild West and marauding red skins. Laughing at the author who obviously hadn't met an educated Indian. I guess he never heard of the Indians helping the first settlers at Plymouth Rock otherwise they might have starved. When the greedy white man came along taking advantage of the Indians, they defended themselves and as in any war there wasn't any mercy shown. At least the book kept him busy until he was home. He lived at the Winthrop House. It felt like home to Brad. Another night on board and they came into their home state.

The whistle blowing and the porter came through calling out, "Chattanooga last stop."

They gathered up their things, the porter put their luggage out on the sidewalk. Brad was looking all around for Quint. He was waiting with the wagon. Sheriff Henry was there with the carriage to drive Mrs. Mary Elizabeth Winthrop, her granddaughter, Ruth and Little Winn to Black Water.

Quint saw them and drove the wagon over. The sheriff came with the carriage to where they were standing.

"Welcome home everyone, glad to see you," Sheriff Henry said.

"Hey, Sheriff, it's good to be home. I never knew how much I missed it until now," Brad replied.

The sheriff came to Mary Elizabeth with the carriage, "Miz Winthrop, welcome to Black Water." He gave her a hand into the carriage.

Ruth and Little Winn stepped in with her. The sheriff climbed in and took the reins. The men loaded the luggage, boxes, and other items which had been ordered on to the wagon. The doctors had ordered some medical equipment and Randy had school items, he and Miss Julie wanted for the school. There was never enough chalk and erasers. The sheriff soon had the horses trotting along the last of the journey to

Black Water. One of these times they would extend a branch rail to Black Water but for now the last twelve miles had to be wagon or carriage.

They went by the Smoky Range Ranch waving as they passed and soon pulled in at Winthrop House.

41

Sheriff Henry pulled in at the front door. He quickly gave Mrs. Winthrop a hand to help her down from the carriage. Next, he helped Ruth down, Little Winn was ready to jump into his arms laughing.

"You little, scamp, you. I missed you in my office." He set him on the porch. Star was happy to see her son and the family home. She was somewhat surprised as Mary Elizabeth stepped up and hugged her. Star had never had this kind of affection shown to her except from her husband, Frank.

"I am so glad to see you again Star. Our little grandson missed you, too."

Star didn't know exactly how to reply to her. Finally she said, "I have fresh made chocolate cake and coffee if you would like or perhaps you would like to settle in first Mrs. Mary Elizabeth?"

"Yes, Dear, I would rather get settled and relax. Then I would love a hot cup of tea and perhaps you might have one of your delicious biscuits with butter and jam. I would enjoy it." Mary Elizabeth hurried to her room and removed her shoes and stockings, and slipped her feet into the moccasins Star had placed by her bed. She changed into her lounging gown and lay down to rest a few minutes. She dozed off.

Ruth holding her son's hand quickly went to see her mother. Little Faun waiting on the porch swing.

"Grandmother, Grandmother, I miss you." Little Winn ran and climbed into her lap hugging her. Ruth leaned and kissed her mother then sat beside her.

"I am so glad to be home, Mother."

"Why don't you take a bath and relax. Then we can talk. I will keep Little Eagle here with me."

'Thanks, Mother I think I will. Then we can have a piece of Mother Star's cake and coffee." She rushed out to her house across the street where Frank was already cleaned up and into his buckskins and moccasins. She quickly bathed, dressed, kissed him. and hurried back to the Winthrop House. The others were in the kitchen at the long table. She quickly poured herself a cup of coffee and took one of the pieces of cake. Little Eagle was in his high chair covered with his chocolate cake. She sat beside her mother.

"This is so good, Mother Star. I am so happy I am home."

Star sat smiling in satisfaction, her son and his family were home again.

Frank and Brad went to Sheriff Henry's office as he had told them the bank was robbed several days ago. They had one of the robbers in the new jail. It now was larger and Quint had made metal bars and windows. It was much more secure than before.

In the evening, everyone gathered in the living room to welcome them, Dr. Young played the piano, Julie kept looking at Brad wondering why he wouldn't ask her to dance, the music was the Blue Danube Waltz. She wondered why people didn't dance here as they did in the city. Randy had been taught to dance when he was in college, but never ask anyone to dance.

Finally Brad went over to Julie, "Would you honor me with this waltz?"

Frank Jr. looked up and thought. Now what's this? His Uncle Brad had been dating Miss Webster. He just sat back wondering about this turn of events.

Randy came over and ask Miss Webster if she would honor him with a dance. Dr. Young was thinking I wish some ne else could play this dammed thing and give me an opportunity to dance.

Unknown to them, Mrs. Brooks who played the hymns on Sundays, also knew other tunes and came to him saying, "Would you like a break Dr. Young? I think I can play Sidewalks of New York its sort of a waltz."

"Yes, a fine choice, perhaps Whitney, will dance with me" The others stood waiting for Mrs. Brooks. She played the piano beautifully and went on into some tune called After the Ball. When she finished they clapped, and thanked her for her part in making the welcome home party a success. They enjoyed iced cold tea and white cake with butterscotch icing.

Red Beard thought, *I guess they didn't know how to do the Highland fling. There weren't any bagpipes anyway.* He said, "Miss Star you are my favorite cook at Winthrop House. No one knows how to bake biscuits and cakes as you."

"Thank you, Red Beard."

They were all ready to turn in for the night. Now they would be having dances at the Winthrop House on Saturday evenings. It seemed Julie and Brad had something in common. Miss Webster seemed to click with the teacher Randy Swain.

Brad really enjoyed Julie with her fresh young attitude about teaching. He was glad she broke the ice inviting him to dance. Saturday nights would never be the same as long as Mrs. Brooks would play the piano for them to dance. Things went along as usual in Black Water. Frank, Jr. thought he would do his dancing to the drums, bells, and chants of the braves during the harvest festival.

42

The town of Black Water had a windmill built with a tank to hold water to supply the little growing town.

When they found the bank had been robbed Frank, immediately wondered if they would recover the money. The thief in jail wouldn't tell where it was and where the others were headed when they ran out of town. Frank had a way of encouraging thieves to talk, if Sheriff Henry would just let him escape.

Frank and Brad assured people who had money in the bank the their money was secured as the Winthrop's would cover it. Frank went to the jail to see what the thief would say.

"Looky you, Mr. big shot Indian. You will never get the money back so don't even think about it."

"What is your name? I don't think we have been introduced."

The thief was taken off guard this Indian speaking to him in this way.

"I think your Sheriff has my name in his office, but I am known as Bad Boy Anderson."

"Well, Bad Boy do you think your friends are going to rescue you from the jail?"

"You better believe it, Injun. They will have me out of Black Water jail before you know it."

"I am looking forward to meeting your friends, Anderson, and welcoming them to Black Water."

"Don't you worry, Injun, they will be here."

Frank went back to Sheriff Henry's office. "Sheriff, he is expecting his friends to attempt a jail break."

"Yes, I know, Frank. I think we can handle it. I have some men deputized including Quint."

"While I am here I would like to be sworn in, too."

"Raise your right hand, Frank."

Frank stood beside the Sheriffs desk raised his right hand.

"Do you, Frank Winthrop, promise to up hold the laws of the state of Tennessee,?"

"Yes, Sheriff, I do."

"By the power vested in me, I now authorize you as a deputy for the town of Black Water, Tennessee." The Sheriff gave Frank a badge to wear so folks would now know he was a deputy.

Several months passed and things were quiet in the town. The deputies weren't fooled into thinking the robbers wouldn't try to free their buddy. The money had been delivered from Boston by Wells Fargo to cover what they had stolen. They hired a guard in the bank. The town was quiet and looked as though everyone was having a siesta. A group of five men rode in and stopped in front of the bank. They looked around and didn't see anyone on the street. They pulled their neckerchiefs over their faces and went into the bank with guns drawn. Unknown to them though Frank, Jr. slipped in his office. When they started to shoot the guard, he returned fire. Frank joined him and before they knew it the five lay on the floor of the bank. The sheriff and his deputies came. They took the bodies to the undertaker. Quint and the others made boxes to bury the robbers at Boot Hill.

The sheriff looked in the saddle bags on their horses still standing in front of the bank. He told his deputies to take the horses to Quint's corral and turn them out. Each saddle bag had a share of the stolen money. It was taken to the jail and counted before being placed in a bank bag and deposited in the bank safe. There would be a hearing for the five who were killed and the matter closed. The one still behind bars would be tried before the circuit judge when he came through.

In the meantime, Sylvia went into labor. Doctors Young and Jones attended the delivery of a six pound baby girl. Everyone in Winthrop House waited to hear the good news.

Mary Elizabeth hugged Star, "Just listen. We have another little grandchild isn't it wonderful?" Mary Elizabeth brought enough diapers to furnish the town. Beautiful little gowns slips booties, undershirts, safety pins. She even bought a perambulator and shipped it by Wells Fargo for the little one.

Frank, Jr. was there on the porch with Strong Bow, to congratulate his-brother-in law on his first baby. In a few minutes Dr. Jones came to the front door.

"Friends. Silvia delivered a beautiful little girl. The baby and mother are both doing just fine. Both are resting and will sleep. Strong Bow if you would like to see her before she goes to sleep come in for a few minutes."

He quickly followed Dr. Jones into the bedroom where Sylvia was resting. Their first born resting in her arms. The doctor stood in the door a moment smiling as Strong Bow stood speechless watching them.

Sylvia said, "Strong Bow isn't our little papoose beautiful?"

Unable to speak, he took her hand kissed it then left the room. Dr. Young called Star to come take the baby and put her in her crib until feeding time.

No amount of words could describe the feeling Mary Elizabeth had seeing the little one. Thinking how lucky she was to have been a part of the child's birth and of birthing the baby's, grandfather, Frank.

The next celebration was held in the acreage behind the Winthrop House. Frank, Jr. wanted to let the town join them with the Indian ceremony. Chief Lone Wolf would be ready to perform the chanting. The braves who now lived in town would once again dress in their buckskins and moccasins around the fire chanting, singing, and dancing to the beat of their ancestor's songs. It was good, Frank, Jr., thought his son now three years old should see the ceremony. His first recollections of it were at Little Eagle's age.

The people of Black Water were delighted to have the ceremony and enjoy the food cooked over the fire. The sheriff rang the school bell telling them of the coming celebration so they would know what to expect when the drums began beating. As it turned out they joined the others at the fire and even danced along with the Indians. It was a joyous occasion and the first of many more to come.

THE END

ABOUT THE AUTHOR

Margaret F. Laing was born in Daytona Beach, FL in 1924 during the great depression. Like many poor young women in the south she received an 8th grade education. During her youth Margaret learned to play guitar. She met her first husband and by age 16 was married. Margaret became a professional musician forming a band, The Daytona Beach Nighthawks. She and her husband had one daughter but as time went on the marriage began to fail and ended in divorce.

Margaret remarried and began better life. She was quite the entrepreneur having owned a well drilling business, thrift store owner/operator. She also finished her high school education, studied Cosmetology and later becoming a CNA. With her second husband she had 3 more children. Margaret's hobbies included, horseback riding, painting, music, writing manuscripts, knitting, crocheting, fishing and nature walks on beach.

www.ingramcontent.com/pod-product-compliance
Lightning Source LLC
Chambersburg PA
CBHW051240250626
47155CB00009B/3102